MW01245866

THE ACCLAIMED SHORT STORIES OF
JOYCELYN WELLS

"What I found in each virtue was a sense of bravery. Proud to follow along and be a part of this transparent journey. It spoke loud and clear, "I am woman, hear me roar." I am an avid reader, and I often run across a lot of "woe is me" tales. It's such a delight to have Joy share, "Wow, it's me." Great read for grown and sexy women everywhere."
-DeNikki Webber

"Just finished reading *The Virtues of Joy*. I truly enjoyed it. I loved how you wrote all the little thoughts and details. And talk about sexy, at times, oh my!! Love the rawness of it. I love how Joy just takes things in stride, not letting it disrupt her being."
-Katie Rolland

"I loved experiencing Joy's tantalizing adventures as a reader. I'm waiting for the movie!"
-anon via amazon

"OK I don't even know where to start with this book. From start to finish this is definitely an attention getter. The stories are amazing. When you read the book, it is as though your best friend is right next to you telling you all the juicy details of her date. It leaves you wanting more. I've never in my life so much wanted to continue to read a book that I felt like I needed to pray about afterwards LOL. 🐵 You definitely want to read this book it's worth your money and time! Believe me she is an amazing writer, and I can't wait until her next book comes out."
-enejyna

"Oh. My. God! This is for the housewives, the ex-wives, future wives, it's for ALLLL of the people!! I absolutely loved it! I love the realness, the beauty found in each man as well as in HERSELF!! The courage of Joy to share these amazing and steamy stories, and her sense of humor. The GIRL POWER!! It's a MUST READ! Joy is amazing!!!
-KaySmile via amazon

"In my opinion, *Shades of Grey* has nothing on Joy's virtues. The eroticism and spiciness within her writing show an outstanding amount of merriment, while many other authors wish they were able and bold enough to add this much steam to their stories on paper. I could imagine everything happening while reading every virtue. Every chapter ended well and then it was on to the next. After I finished the last chapter, I found myself longing for more."
-Mina Smith, author

BOOKS BY JOYCELYN WELLS

Compilation of Short Stories

The Virtues of Joy
More Virtues of Joy
Mor3 Virtues of Joy

A Virtue of Joy

Authenticity

Tales of Chance & Joy

The Weekend of Traveling Roses

JOYCELYN WELLS

DEATH BY A WEDDING

SHAPE PUBLISHING
ATLANTA | TAMPA

SHAPE Publishing
www.myshape.solutions

Originally published in paperback in 2022

SHAPE Publishing is a division of mySHAPE.solutions, Inc.

For my mother, Joyce Elizabeth Johnson,
the unadulterated embodiment of love, hope and fashion.

For my dear friend, Natalie Martin, for every moment I couldn't, your journey reminded me that I could.
#BadAssNat #200strong

To my forever love, thank you for loving me, unconditionally.

DEATH
BY A
WEDDING

Order of Service

Joycelyn Wells

TORRENTIAL DOWNPOUR

Death By A Wedding

Lord, I have never in all my years seen, or heard, for that matter, rain fall like this. Please keep us safe. I whispered. "Amen!"

Matt stammered, "Huh? Not now. I can't talk right now."

I didn't respond. I knew he couldn't talk. Hell, he can barely drive on a sunny day. I know this storm has him completely fucked up. I looked over at him. Was he even breathing? He didn't look like it. I wanted to say something, but I didn't. Anything I said would be blown out of proportion. Somedays, I swear it seems like my breathing is an inconvenience to him. I decided to forego any reference to his driving in this rain. He's fully aware that his driving abilities are mediocre. But I can tell, today he's more afraid than anything. And to be honest, so was I. This drive would be challenging for me too!

Hi! I'm Johanna Williams Monroe. Matt and I have been married for six years. We met in undergraduate school; we were the last two at the party. I mean that in the most literal sense. It was a house party that I went to with my girlfriend Allison. Everyone was gone and I was sitting on the sofa waiting for her. She was in the back with her guy Cal. Just as I had snuggled under a blanket on the couch, comfortable with the idea that I'd probably be sleeping there for the rest of the night, Matt entered the living room. I sat up immediately. I knew Cal but I had never met this guy.

He flashed a giant smile. So big that you could see that there was a gap smack dab in the middle of his teeth. I don't know why but I felt like it added to his charm. The perfect space, with straight white teeth standing guard on each side.

"Hey! I'm Xavier from Chi-town, Soufside."

Lying ass. He was from the Soufside of a country ass town in the Confederate South. His southern drawl contradicted his statement. He probably had family that migrated to Chicago. But hey? Who am I to judge? I nodded and forced a smile.

"Where you from?"

"Marietta..." I looked for something in his face to indicate familiarity. There was nothing, So I continued, "uh, Georgia. It's north of Atlanta."

"Oh, I know where it is. I know plenty of people in Georgia. And I know 'bout Mayretta too." Mayretta is the urban slang of Marietta. I raised an eyebrow, maybe he does know a little about Mayretta. I tuned in to his ramblings. He rattled off random statistics about Georgia. "Did you know there are 159 counties in Georgia."

"Seriously? No, I didn't know that."

He continued, "Mayretta isn't the largest city but it's growing. It's progressive."

"You don't say?"

"Where did you attend high school?"

"Marietta High School."

He turned to look at me. "Oh, you didn't go to school in Cobb County?"

"Well, I guess I did, Marietta is in Cobb County."

"Is Marietta High a Cobb County School?"

"No, it's a Marietta City School."

So, you are from the city?"

"Yes."

"Wow, well ain't that som'thin." He thought for a minute, "I ain't never met anyone from Marietta proper."

I stuck out my hand, "Well, hi. I'm Johanna. My friends call me Jo."

"Well, hi Jo. Pleased ta meecha."

The music was low, a TV flashed in the corner and Matt's boisterous energy filled the room. With there being no other distractions, Matt and I continued to occupy each other's time. We talked about politics, Black American or African American, Black folks in the United States, Martin Luther King, Jr., or Malcolm X? Fishing or dancing? You name it we talked about it. By the time the light from the sun illuminated the living room, I would've sworn that he was the smartest person I had ever met.

I asked about his favorite books. He replied, "I'm not a big reader of books." I reflected on our conversation; clearly, he loved facts and information; yet, he didn't read books. *Interesting.* I wondered where he got his information from. "Well, I have a book that I think you should read."

"Yeah?"

"*The Invisible Man* by Ralph Ellison."

"I'll have to get my hands on a copy."

"You should. You can get it at any library."

Before we could get into any other topics, Allison finally emerged from the back. "Hey gurrl! I've got so much to…"

I interrupted her. "Allison. Finally! Hey! You ready?" I needed to cut her off before she said some crazy shit. With Allison, you never knew what was gonna come outta her mouth!

"Yeah, let me get my shoes." She was talking nonstop, as she was putting on her sneakers. She didn't even see Matt sitting there. "What have you been doing? I thought you would be asleep or gone."

"I was going to go to sleep but that didn't happen. I've been here chatting with Xavier. Do you know him? He's from Chicago… Soufside" Sarcasm dripped from my words.

As I was finishing my statement, Allison peered into the living room. Cal appeared from the hallway. They, Allison and Cal, both exclaimed at the same time, "Xavier?"

I looked at the gentleman who had so graciously kept me company all night with his tales and random knowledge. "Oh, I'm sorry. You said Xavier, correct?"

Everyone started laughing. Clearly, I was outside of the joke.

Cal stopped laughing, "Matt, why are you still here? And, more importantly, why are you lying to the young lady?"

"Matt?" I questioned.

He looked at me, sheepishly, then back at Cal, "First of all, why are y'all calling me out? Xavier is the name I use for the lay...dies." There was a pause between the syllables for emphasis. He continued, "Second, I couldn't leave her alone while y'all were otherwise engaged. Someone needed to keep her company, why couldn't it be me?"

Allison blushed at the "otherwise engaged" comment. Cal reached out to touch her. *Oh ok, I see where this could go... again.* I shook my head and picked up my purse. "Allison, you comin' or staying?"

Allison grabbed her purse. I waited at the door while Cal covered her in hugs and kisses. Cal and Matt or Xavier walked out behind us. As we got into the car, we said, "goodnight or good morning." They closed our doors and laughter filled the car.

"You've gotta give details! I want to know everything. What happened? Spill it!"

"Ok, ok, first..."

Allison talked nonstop all the way through breakfast. She had a great time. And I enjoyed reliving the night with her. I have to admit, I did think about my time spent with Xavier or Matt, whatever his fucking name is. He was smart as hell.

But it was whatever, good-bye and good riddance Xavier? Matt? Whoever the fuck you are... Ughh!

That memory prompted me to look over at his scary ass. All these years later and here he was, gripping the steering well so tight, like his life depended on it. Well, honestly, all our lives depended on it. His face was tense, and eyes were squinted. For the life of me, I don't know why I felt the urge to say something about his driving or the weather or anything else just to fuck with him. Especially since, he's been such an ass these few months. Hell, who am I kidding, he's always an ass. I decided against all of it, he wouldn't be able to handle it and I'm not risking our safety in the event that he has a meltdown.

How did I end up here, you ask? From chatting all night with a poser pretending to be from Chi-town to being married to that very person and raising two adorable little girls. Well, the story isn't amazing; though, it's real. Matt was kind and smart. He was also available. I was available. That's the story. We were the two people that attended events alone and, eventually, ended up together. He would call, "hey Jo, are you going to the football game?"

"Yeah."

"Cool, I'll see you there." "Hey, Jo, will you be at happy hour?"

"Yeah."

"Ok. See you there."

As I think about it, we never really dated. We just fell into a rhythm of togetherness. We were comfortable in each other's presence.

And that's all there is to say about that!

Matt's always been easy on the eyes. Even today, dressed to a tee in his tux. Thoughts of our first ball, flashed through my mind. His skin was so smooth and chocolate. When he smiled, I could see forever. He owned that gap. I believe on many occasions he displayed it intentionally. It was his shit! From the moment I saw it, I just knew he inherited it from someone, and his kids would inherit it from him.

I turned in my seat to check on the girls. They were sitting rigid and wide-eyed. Jacquelyn leaned forward as far as she could in her booster seat. I reached my arm across the seat, just enough to brush her face with my fingers. Her lips parted and her dad's smile appeared. I knew it... the gap. I smiled back.

Janise, in her car seat, continued to look out the window at the rain.

"Janise? Where's your baby?"

She didn't turn around or say anything. She just lifted it from the space between her car seat and the door.

"Oh, ok."

"Mommy?"

"Yes, Jacquelyn?"

"This rain is crazy."

It wasn't a question. I just nodded in agreement. "We will be there soon. Everything will be fine."

"Y'all need to stop all that talking. I can't concentrate."

Jacquelyn's eyes widened. She recognized his tone. Hell, we all recognized his grumpy ass tone. *He was never able to process more than one thing as a time.* She reached over to take Janise's hand. Janise didn't flinch, she just allowed her hand to be enveloped by her sister. Jacquelyn would always be her protector. They would take care of each other. Sisters.

Matt was such a stickler for appearances. I'm sure that I would've pulled over 20 minutes ago. Though, Matt? He would never. I mean, what's the rush? We are already late as hell.

We were in a processional of cars, all going to the same place. Which wasn't a bad idea because we were all visiting from out of town. Hell, in this torrential downpour, we need to be following someone who knew where we were going. The map wouldn't have done us any good this time, I couldn't read the street signs if I tried.

Matt and his "council" were all following each other to the venue. They have been referring to themselves as "The Council" since they met in grad school. So, there's no way in hell that he would be so bold as to pull over for his safety or that of his family. We could all perish for the sake of "The Council."

The girls and I needed a distraction. Just as I was about to ask Matt, if we could turn on the radio, brake lights illuminated in front of us. We all jerked forward then back. The blinker on the car in front of us, signaled a right turn. The rain continued to fall in sheets. I leaned forward to look for any type of signage. I couldn't see anything.

We continued to ease forward until it was our turn to enter the parking lot.

"I guess this is the place. Can you read the sign?"

Matt replied, "Not yet, as soon as I make this right, we should be able to see it."

Glancing at Matt, I noticed his hands had relaxed a bit. Cool. We have reached our destination. I turned on the radio. He looked at me.

"Jesus Matt, we are here already. A little music will help us all relax."

He didn't reply. Just continued to inch forward towards the entrance.

The girls were looking around. I don't know what they were thinking but my thoughts were on this rain letting up before we got out of the van. Hopefully, we'd get a bit of a reprieve. One thing for sure, I knew that I wasn't getting out with my girls in this mess. We would not be messing up our perfect dresses or hair. And we had to redo our hair this morning, so nope we will not be messing it up before we get to where we are going. *Maybe there's a parking garage? That would be ideal.*

"Do you see a valet or parking garage?"

Matt asked, "I can't see anything yet. What does that sign say?"

I looked. "What sign, I can't see anything."

"Over there," he pointed. I felt him grab my chin. He tried to turn my head. I flinched by I didn't turn away. Now, I know I already told his ass not to touch me. He remembered because he moved his hand and said, "the sign over to the left, Jo. The one on the building."

"Yeah, I see it but..."

"Jo, can you read it?"

I leaned forward as to get a closer look. "Hang on a sec. Oh my god! Matt..."

I looked at him and then back towards the sign. "Do you recognize anybody's car? Did we follow the right car?"

Matt answered, "Yes."

"Is this the right address?"

"Yes."

"Oh my God! Are you sure 'cause this is a fucking..."

He finished my sentence. "Funeral Home."

We just stared at each other. I reached to turn the radio down. He continued to inch forward until he found an available parking space. There were so many cars in the lot. Where did all these cars come from?

"This isn't right."

"What the fuck, Matt?"

The rain fell even harder.

6 Months Earlier

THE INVITATION

Matt was talking as he entered the house. I was cleaning the kitchen. When I heard the door open, I looked in on the girls. They were playing a game in the living room. He was still talking when I picked up the broom.

"Jo! Jo!"

I turned to look at him. "You talking to me?"

"Who else do you think I'm talking to?"

Hell, I didn't know. He never talks to me. I stopped sweeping. "Oh, I didn't know. What did you say?"

He just looked at me with that look of his. Finally, he spoke. "We're going to Miami."

"Ok." I started sweeping again.

He continued, "Adam proposed to Alicia. They are getting married in June."

"Oh, that's nice. It's about time. How old is their baby now?"

"He's almost two months."

He droned on about 'The Council' and how they would all be groomsmen in the wedding. I continued to sweep and nod, as if he had my undivided attention.

"I figured we could make a long weekend of it, you know? Come back on Monday."

"Sounds wonderful. Do you need for me to make your hotel reservations? Are you sharing a room with someone? King bed or two doubles?"

"What?"

"Do you want me to reserve your hotel room?" *Did he not hear me?*

He paused. Eventually, I looked at him. He was staring at me. *"What?"*

"We are going."

It took my mind a minute to compute *we*. "Oh, you want me to go?"

"Yes, you and the girls."

I smiled on the inside. *Whoa! He wants us to go with him to Miami.* "Oh ok."

"There will be a lot of important people there. I can't go by myself. I need for my family to be there."

"Aha!" I knew it, *always a fucking angle.* I started sweeping again.

"Make sure you request the days off."

I looked at the girls again then him and nodded in his direction.

"When I get more information, I'll let you know."

"Ok."

My thoughts were all over the place. *He never wants to do anything with us. His motives are always self-serving.* By the time I finished, I had come to this conclusion... the council must all be bringing their girlfriends.

Whatever the reason, I'm down for a trip to Miami.

TOGETHER
WITH THEIR FAMILIES

Adam
&
Alicia

WE INVITE YOU TO JOIN OUR WEDDING

Sat | **May** **23** | 1998

ONE O'CLOCK IN THE AFTERNOON
LIBERTY CITY BAPTIST - MIAMI

Reception Immediately Following
Reflections Event Hall

PERFECT DRESSES

Over the next few months, all the talk in our home was about the wedding. Drive or fly? Hotel room or suite? We were all excited for different reasons, of course.

For Matt? His boy was getting married. As for me, I was excited to be going somewhere. Hell, any damn where!

Every chance I got, I was searching for the perfect dresses for me and my girls. We had to wear the same colors, of course. Now, don't get me wrong, we, the girls and I go places, but Matt? He's perfectly content staying at home. So, for him to be hyped about going to Miami, "The Bottom," as it is referred to in all the songs, is a huge change from his normal routine.

Some background, we lived in the city in which he grew up. His parents were right around the corner. He knew everyone. So, it's not uncommon for him to not want to go anywhere. Everything he ever needed was right here in this space. It's funny as I look back on it, I encouraged this mess. *"Come on Matt, it would be great to live near your*

family. Your parents can spend time with the girls. Don't you think it's a good idea?"

Truth be told, 'we' didn't need help with the girls, I needed help. Matt didn't do a damn thing. Matt did Matt. Once I finally wrapped my mind around that fact, my requests for him and for us to do came to a screeching halt. I mean seriously how many times would I subject myself to his brutal ass 'no'?

Whew, I digress. Let me get back to planning our trip to Miami for his wedding.

Macy's? Sears? Dillards? Burdines? Listen, I looked everywhere. As you can tell, this was before the internet took off. I mean yes, there was catalog shopping but there was nothing like walking through the stores, touching the fabric, and explaining to the salesperson what you envisioned for the day. In our town, Gainesville, FL, I continued coming up short. It could be the perfect dress but the wrong sizes or they only had one in stock. Or the right sizes but the dresses were downright homely... as hell.

"Ughh!" I started stressing. Lord knows the last thing I wanted to hear was Matt's mouth about not being ready. *Wait. Would he have even noticed?* Here I go, interjecting thoughts or words for him. Well, whatever, his response, I didn't fucking want to hear it.

So, I called the guru of shopping. My mother. She was, by far, the most stylish person I have ever known. When I was a little girl, she used to paint her nails every night to match her outfit for the next day. So, trust me when I say she paid attention to the details, 'cause she did!

Luckily for me, a few years ago, she and my sister moved to Jacksonville, FL from our home in Marietta, GA. Her reasoning had something to do with her job. However, in my mind, her moving equated to her being closer to me and the girls. It's what I needed.

"Hello?"

"Hey Ma. How are you?"

"Hey, Johanna. I'm good. You? My girls?"

"We are all doing well."

"Good."

"Ma, I can't find us anything to wear to that wedding in Miami. It's in three weeks and I have nothing."

"Oh damn!"

"What?"

"I was just in Dillard's and saw some dresses that would be perfect for the girls."

From whiny to perky, "Really?"

"Yes." She went on to describe the dresses. "The background was white with a pastel floral arrangement on the sleeves and around the hem. I believe the sash was turquoise... or was it lavender?"

"Uh I don't know. And it really doesn't matter. We just need dresses."

"They were beautiful. Perfect for a summer wedding."

Ok, I have to explain, my mom saying, "summer wedding." It doesn't mean a wedding in the summer, it's in reference to the appropriate attire for a specific time frame. For instance, some people would reference September as summertime but the rule for white after Labor Day would deem those particular dresses as inappropriate. Since Easter has passed, I'm thinking that according to *Ma's Rules of Etiquette* these dresses are "perfect for a summer wedding."

I know it's torturous; however, I was raised by this woman, so I understand the meaning behind her words.

"Were you in the toddler section, Ma?"

"Yes, of course."

"Why were you looking there?"

"Well, I was walking by going to the shoe department and the dresses caught my eye. So, I stopped and looked around. Is that ok with you?"

"Yes, I was just wondering how you ended up in the kids section."

"Well, do you want me to go see if they have the right sizes for Jacquelyn and Janise?"

"That would be amazing. Jacquelyn is a 4T and Janise is a 2T."

"What about you?"

"What about me what?"

"What size dress are you wearing these days?"

"I'll find something for me. Will you please just grab the dresses for the girls?"

"Well, if I'm out shopping for them, I might as well look for you too."

I sighed. She's right. She will put that ensemble together like nobody's business. "Ok, Ma, I'm wearing a 12."

"A 12?" I could hear the sarcasm in her voice.

"Ok, a 14. I was hoping to be in a 12 before the wedding."

"Hm, I see, I'll look for both, just in case."

"Thanks, Ma. We will come over next weekend to try everything on. Is that ok?"

"Honey, ya'll can come anytime. Is Matt coming?"

I fought the urge to say *maybe*. I was reminded that I stopped covering for him a couple of years ago. "No."

"Alright then, I'll go get the dresses in the morning. If they don't have the right sizes, I'll have them check one of the other stores."

"Thanks so much, Ma."

"Anything for my babies."

When I hung up that phone, I released a sigh of relief. *"Yes, Ma, yes!"* There was no doubt in my mind that she would choose the perfect dresses for us. It was her thing. Matt walked in the room as I was doing my little celebratory dance.

"What are you all excited about?" His grumpy ass tone was enough to cast shade over my sunshine.

"Nothing, just got off the phone with my mother."

"And you are happy about it?"

Ugh, he's such a downer. "It was nothing really."

"It didn't look like nothing."

"It was nothing. The girls and I are gonna go for a short visit on Friday."

"When y'all coming back?"

I used to think that he was asking because he didn't want us to be gone long. Usually, I would rush back Friday night or first thing Saturday morning.

I mumbled, "Late Friday or... I'm not sure."

"I may not be here when y'all get home. The boys and I are getting together..."

I cut him off, "fine."

As he spoke, I realized that he was just trying to figure out how much time he would have to himself. No need to explain anything to me. I had become accustomed to knowing that when he started with, *the council and I are...* that meant he would be out until whenever. As I turned to walk out of the room, I heard Matt say, "Jo?" I stopped but I didn't turn around.

"Yes?"

"How are the plans coming for our trip?"

He wanted to make sure that I wasn't upset about his plans to go out this weekend.

"Everything is coming along just fine. I was able to book the room. The space would be good for the girls and not to mention there's a huge tub. I figure the girls can play in it." I made a mental note to pack some water-friendly toys.

"Sounds good."

"We are booked from Thursday to Monday, alright?"

"Thursday? Everyone else isn't leaving until Friday."

I turned to face him. *Fuck everyone else. I'm talking about me and mine.*

"Yes, Thursday. You said a long weekend."

"I was talking about leaving on Monday, not going on Thursday. It doesn't make sense to get there that early."

"Get to Miami early? Miami is always ready besides we are the only ones traveling with kids."

"What does that have to do with anything?"

I looked in his eyes and realized he was serious. He didn't have a fucking clue.

"It would be best for us to arrive early. We need to get the girls acclimated and allow them an opportunity to rest. The drive alone will be taxing. Besides, it wouldn't be fair to the bride and groom or their guests to pop in with two restless toddlers on the evening before the wedding."

He looked thoughtful for a minute. Maybe he needed to talk it over with "the council," to see if it were ok for him to make a move without them. Alright, alright, that wasn't nice, I'm sure you can hear the resentment in my words. But I was serious...

"Ok, if that's what needs to happen to make sure this weekend is perfect then we will leave Thursday around noon."

"Perfect for who? You sound like you are getting married?"

"You know what I mean."

"What will make the weekend perfect is that the couple says, 'I do'. We are coming along to join in the celebration."

"Nah, it's more than that for me."

"How so?"

"Adam has gotten offers from some of the most prestigious firms in the country."

"What does that have to do with you?"

"I'll have the opportunity to network and possibly work with those firms in the future. So, I need for our shit to be on point."

I stared at him for a minute searching for anything that made sense. There was nothing. "Ok, I completely understand. You need for your family to present as perfect, in hopes of wooing the firms that are courting Adam. Gotcha."

"Whatever Jo, we are all excited about his wedding. And that's that."

"We?"

"You know what I mean."

"Cool. Anything else?"

"Huh?"

"Do you need anything else from me right now?"

"No."

I nodded my head and walked off. *What kind of silly shit was that?*

The rest of the week went by in a blur. I spoke with my mother; she was able to purchase the dresses in the correct sizes. She confirmed the color of the sash... turquoise. Once we arrived in Jacksonville on Friday, we would look for a matching dress for me.

While I was excited about going to Miami. Matt was excited about the wedding. On several occasions during the week, I overheard him planning activities with the council. None of his plans included us, other than the wedding. Which was fine, I'd make plans for us. Lord knows I'm not going to be held hostage in a hotel for the weekend.

I wonder what we talked about before Adam announced his wedding. I'm just saying because for the last few months that's all any of us could talk about. All cynicism aside, I do love a good wedding. There's just something about two people declaring their love to each other.

Death By A Wedding

We've attended two other weddings in Miami. Matt was a groomsman in David's wedding. They were childhood friends. When I tell you that the only thing that could've made that wedding better was if they left in a helicopter! You better believe me. Talking about luxurious. It was all everything.

For Sonya's wedding, I was her maid of honor. I knew her from the dorms. We lived on the same floor. I was drawn to her because she was from Miami and had a little girl. Her wedding was south of Miami, in Homestead. It was beautiful, sweet, and elegant. However, in the surrounding areas there were remnants of destruction. This was my firsthand experience with the turmoil caused by hurricane season,

As I'm thinking about it, Matt and I definitely had a wedding season. Prior to having kids, it seems like we went to at least one wedding or reception or both each year. Now, it's a bit more stressful because, I'm responsible for more than just me. I'm hoping this wedding will be good for us. Outside of the kids, we don't seem to have anything else to talk about. He seems pretty content with his life with me on the outside. While I'm hell bent on building a life for all of us. I'm happy that we are at least talking for now. I'm hopeful this will be good for both of us. I'll make sure to pack something special for him.

We made it to my mom's house early Friday afternoon. It's important to beat the traffic especially when kids are involved. The less time spent in a car, the better. I learned that early in the parenting process. Mom was happy to see us. She's always happy to see us. I can always relax into myself when I'm with my mom. She engages with the girls which relieves me of a bit of 'mommy'ing.

"Oooh my girls are here! Jacquelyn! Janise! And my big girl, Mommy!" The first thing I did once I entered her house was pour a glass of wine. "Yay Cabernet! Thanks Mom."

She looked me dead in the eyes, as if she knew something that I had yet to share, "How are you holding up baby?"

I stammered, "Huh? Uh, I'm good."

It was weird. It was like I wanted to give a different answer. Her eyes expected the answer that I didn't give. I smiled. "We are all good." I changed the subject. "The ride over was quick. We must have timed the traffic perfectly."

"Are y'all hungry or thirsty?" I raised my wine glass and mouthed, "I'm good."

"No ma'am."

"No"

"Say no ma'am, Janise."

I mumbled, "she's fine."

Jacquelyn responded, "but mommy that's rude. Ma is a grown-up."

"Yes, you are correct. Janise, it's no ma'am."

Begrudgingly, Janise uttered, "No ma'am, not thirsty or hungry."

"Well, that's fine for now. Y'all let me know if y'all change your minds." She began to walk away.

I shooed them along to keep in step with Ma.

She talked and walked through the house. We all followed. Eventually, we ended up in her dressing room. As promised, we saw the most perfect dresses for the wedding.

"Oh, my goodness Ma! These are beautiful!" I removed one from the rack. "What do you think Jacquelyn?"

"It's a princess dress."

Ma smiled at her, lovingly, "the perfect dresses for our princesses."

Janise couldn't care less. She was trying to put on Ma's shoes. She loved to walk through the house in them. It didn't take Ma long to figure out that she needed to keep her favorites out of Janise's reach.

"Ooohhh I'm so thankful for you. Now, I've gotta grab something for me. I'm so ready for this wedding to be over. It's all we ever talk about."

"At least you are talking."

"Huh? What did you say?"

"Oh, at least you are talking."

I thought for a moment that I should dodge that comment but hell she was right. "Yeah, that's what I said... about the wedding at least."

She kept moving stuff around and talking at the same time, "I pulled out a couple of dresses for you to try. If you don't like either of these, we can go to the mall."

"Mom, you have the best closet. You should be a professional shopper!"

Laughing, she replied, "I am."

"You know what I mean but hey whatever you are doing is working perfectly for me."

I twirled around while holding both dresses in front of me. "I'll start with this one."

"That's my first choice too. Go on and try it. If you like it, you can have it."

"No, that's ok. I'll just borrow it."

"For now, just try it on."

"Okay, okay," I muttered.

As I walked into the bathroom, I heard mom say, "So, those are your shoes for today? We need to find you a purse." I laughed 'cause I knew exactly who she was talking to... Janise. She would be clunking around in those heels for the rest of the day.

I removed my clothes so I could try on this beautiful dress. *What is this taffeta? Silk?* Whatever it was I could tell it was expensive. Before

I slipped into the dress, I looked at my reflection in the mirror. *Will I ever be beautiful again? 'Pretty but not sexy.' I believe those were the words Matt used. Maybe if I was both Matt would want to talk to me? I used to be sexy, didn't I?*

Flashbacks of dancing on speakers, laughing and flirting filled my mind. *Yeah, I was beautiful and sexy before. Where's that Jo?* My thoughts were interrupted by a knock on the door. I reached for the dress. "Yes?" and, as if I didn't know, "Who is it?"

"Mommy, it's me."

Jacquelyn. I could hear soft thuds across the carpet. Janise was working it out in her shoes.

"Ok, me who?"

Giggles.

"Come on mommy, let me see your perfect dress."

"Give me another minute, I'll be right out."

As I was slipping into the dress, I noticed the tag. *My goodness, she's never worn it. I definitely can't keep it.* It slipped on like a glove. *I want this dress. Sweet Jesus.* It was gorgeous. Hell, I was gorgeous, and I felt... sexy. *Matt will love this.* I opened the door.

"Well, what do you think?"

We were all speechless because my mom had dressed my girls in their dresses. Finally, she spoke, "Yes, I knew this dress would fit you. I grabbed it as soon as I saw it on the rack."

"Ma, I thought this was yours?"

"Nope, I never said that. I said, I pulled a couple of dresses out for you. I didn't say out from where."

"Ma!"

"I got it for you. Well, at least now, we know which one to return."

"Mommy you look so pretty."

"So do you Jacquelyn. Just look at you Janise, you already have the shoes to match."

"Speaking of shoes, want to go to the mall? Y'all all need new shoes and purses to match..."

"Our perfect dresses."

OUR WEDDING

We left Mom's on Sunday; my intention was to leave on Saturday, but we were all having such a good time. One more day wouldn't hurt. Besides Matt didn't call even once. He was probably having a good time too. Knowing him, he probably didn't notice that we weren't there anyway.

I pushed that negative thought away. I smiled to myself as I tried to predict his reaction when he saw my dress. I went back and forth between showing it to him when we got home or saving it for the day of the wedding. If he asks, I'll show him. If he doesn't, I'll wait. Fair.

The thought of saving it until the wedding brought back some sweet memories of our wedding day. We were so young, naive and optimistic. This probably sounds like many twenty-somethings getting married way too young and for the wrong reasons. No one was forcing us to get married. We wanted to be together. In all honesty, we believed that our love was truly enough.

We had a small church wedding in North Georgia. My daddy officiated our ceremony. Thinking back on it, I believe he married all his kids off at some point. There were seven of kids. Hell, if I remember correctly, he even married a couple of my brothers two or three times.

Probably all for free, he could've made a grip if he would've charged the standard fee. Too funny! I'll make sure to mention it the next time I speak to him. At some point, he put the hammer down and said, "no more." He felt like we weren't taking our vows seriously. Although, we would have all argued our intention, he was right. We were all young as hell and didn't have a single clue!

Anyway, as for me, I wanted a winter wedding. I can still see it. The church decorated with 8-foot Douglas Firs. Each tree would don twinkling lights and drapings of mauve and ivory tulle, my signature wedding colors. If we were lucky the lawn would be covered in freshly fallen snow. Ohh, it would have been a beautiful winter wonderland. To this day, I'm still in love with the idea of that wedding.

So, we got married in July. I know, I know, if I loved the idea of a winter wedding so much, why did we get married in July? Well, one day in late spring Matt came to me and said, "do you want to get married or not?"

"Of course, I do. I said 'yes', didn't I?"

He took my hands into his. "Well, why do we have to wait? Let's just go get married."

"What about our winter wedding? Our family? Our friends?"

"Do you need all that? And planning for everyone is going to be expensive."

I didn't need it, but I wanted it. *All of it.* I could feel my tears filling the wells of my eyes.

"But Matt, I really want to have the winter wedding. I've dreamed about it my whole life."

You agreed and everyone is already in planning mode."

I felt him squeeze my hands. I tried not to blink or anything. I could not avert my eyes or anything because if I did, the tears would flow, and I would have to admit that heart ached.

He stared into my eyes and smiled. "We can do that for our vow renewal ceremony in 10 years. Right now, I just want to get married to you."

Romantic, right? How could I say 'no' to his reasoning? Or to that gap, standing ever so boldly within his smile?" I trusted him and his words. I'd get my winter wedding eventually.

And that's how it happened. Our winter wedding was changed to a summer wedding just like that. I remember my mom almost stroking out when I told her that plans had changed.

"Are you pregnant?"

"No."

"Are you sure?"

"Yes, I'm sure. Matt just wants to hurry and get married."

"Well, what about you? What do you want?"

"I'm fine with what Matt wants."

"I need to make some calls. I'll call you back."

Now, my uncle on the other hand, was not pleased at all. Not just about the dates changing but the whole idea just rubbed him the wrong way.

"Gnat," he calls me Gnat, "you haven't even finished school yet."

"I know. I'm going to finish. I promise."

"Don't you think that you should both give this engagement a little more time. What's the rush?"

"We are ready now. It'll be fine."

I needed his blessing. We needed his blessing.

My mother went into a shopping frenzy. Bridesmaids' dresses, wedding cake, hors d'oeuvres and flowers... She was so clutch in this process. As for my dress, I found it at a local boutique. It was a beautiful off-white, A-line dress, knee length, and bustling with layers of tulle and chiffon. I fell in love with it immediately. What's even better, it was on sale and the display was my size. Just a couple of minor alterations, which I hand stitched, then off to the dry cleaners. It was perfect. *Something new.*

We didn't have time to send out invitations. Matt and I called our closest friends and told them that we were changing the date. Some would make it, others would not. Fortunately, his best man, Cal, and my maid of honor, Natasha, both lived in the area. They would be there and that meant the world to us.

On our wedding day, I was excited and nervous and scared, all at the same time. I hadn't seen Matt since the day before. I was hopeful that he didn't have too much to drink at his bachelor's party. Know what else? I prayed that he *would* show up. I'm sure it was just my nerves, but the thought did cross my mind.

I would ride to the church with Natasha. Before I left the house, my mom was still attending to the smallest details. She called me to her room. She told me that I she loved me. "I know Mom."

She went on to say, "I was saving this for a special occasion. I guess this is as special of an occasion as it gets."

"Yes, it is pretty special. My wedding day." She paused and turned to look on her dresser. I was listening and waiting. When she came back, she held a square green gift box. I inhaled deeply because I recognized the box. My heart raced there is no way she's giving this to me. This box had a been a part of her jewelry collection for my whole life. It was special.

Hesitantly, she removed the top from the box. There was a square of cotton covering the contents. She seemed to move in slow motion as she removed this. Her tears began to flow. So, of course, mine didn't hesitate to follow. We just stood there silently. It took her a moment to gather her words.

"Johanna?"

"Yes, ma'am?"

"First, I'd like for you to wear this today on your wedding day."

She held out the most beautiful single strand pearl bracelet. I knew what it was, I had coveted it for years. I was overwhelmed at the thought of being able to wear it. I extended my right wrist, and she placed the bracelet on securing it with a clasp of diamonds and gold. We admired it. It was so elegant.

I spoke first, "thank you, Mom."

"You are welcome, baby."

"Mom?"

"Hm?" She was lost in her own thoughts.

"Second?"

"What baby?"

"You said, first, right?"

"Oh yeah."

"Well, what's second?" She reached out to touch the bracelet. Her hand tightened around my wrist.

"And Second," she smiled. "I want my shit back!"

"Mom? Are you kidding?"

"Nope." We both laughed uncontrollably.

"Bye mom."

"See you at the church." *Borrowed.*

My sister would ride with her, and they would pick up the cake and flowers. My future in-laws had arrived the night before. They would go directly to the church. The day was filled with chaos and excitement.

I can't remember who came to get me from my dad's study to tell me it was time. When that door opened, it felt like I took my first breath all day. My uncle was waiting for me. He was going to walk me down the aisle and present me to my husband. He had tears. I had tears. We took a moment to collect ourselves. He handed me a linen handkerchief embroidered with blue flowers. I found out later that had belonged to my grandmother. *Something old & blue.*

My maid of honor stood ready for processional, along with my youngest sister, who would serve as my Jr. Bridesmaid. And that's it. That was my wedding party. Me, Natasha and Nevaeh. They looked so beautiful in their mauve dresses.

The music from the organ filled the foyer of the church, the doors opened, Nevaeh entered the sanctuary first then Natasha. The doors were closed again. We listened for the music to change, the first note to *Here Comes The Bride.* My uncle looked at me and crooked his arm to make a space for mine. I stepped to him and slipped my arm into his. The doors opened and we began our walk to the altar.

Believe me when I say, it was the longest walk I'd ever taken. Even today, I promise, it still seems like forever. I looked around the church as I walked. There were so many faces. Though, I only recognized a few. I looked towards the altar. There was Matt and that amazing smile. I relaxed a little. Cal handed Matt a handkerchief, Matt took it and placed it in his tuxedo pocket. He was ready.

Once I arrived at the altar, I noticed that my dad had been crying too. Lord, we were all a weeping mess. Matt held my hands tight. He wanted me to look him in his eyes. I did. He mouthed, "Are you ok?"

I nodded yes. "I'm fine."

He looked at my dad, smiled and said, "Alright Reverend. You ready?"

The congregation, filled with family and my dad's church family, laughed. Which prompted laughter from all of us. He certainly knew how to lighten the mood. Just like that we were married in July.

I allowed myself to get lost in the nostalgia as we drove home. I made a note to mention our wedding ceremony to Matt. I wonder if he remembers how sweet and sentimental the day was. *How did we lose that?*

I reached up to press the garage door opener. I prayed that Matt would be home. He wasn't. Ironically, I breathed a sigh of relief. I looked into the rear-view mirror; the girls were asleep. It's funny that during the whole ride, I was lost in the thought of our wedding. I didn't even miss the banter and noise associated with their playfulness.

Joycelyn Wells

I dismissed the wedding thoughts. That was almost nine years ago. According to Matt's plan, we should be renewing our vows next year.

Hmph would I renew what we have? Would he?

"We are home. Time to wake up."

43

YEAH

The afternoon sped right along. By the time we unpacked, cooked, ate dinner, cleaned the kitchen, and played a couple of games, it was nearly bedtime. Matt hadn't made it home yet.

I wanted to call but I didn't even know where he was. Hell, you know what's worse than that? I didn't want to bother him and I sure as hell didn't want him to bother me. He had this way of making sure you knew you were a bother without actually saying you were a bother. Something about his tone or lackluster responses always let you know. He did this rubbing thing with his fingers like he was irritated. So, fuck it. He knows where he is. And I'm sure he's alright wherever that is.

"Alright girls, it's time for bed. Jacquelyn will you please start the bath water?"

"But Mommy, I'm not ready."

"I know but it is getting late, and tomorrow is Monday."

"School tomorrow?"

"Yes, school for you and off to Mrs. Perry's for Janise."

She didn't reply. Finally, she's getting into the hang of having regular school days and some responsibilities.

"Come here Janise, let's get undressed."

"Bath time!"

"Yes, princess, bath time."

We went through the process of playing and bathing. *I'll need to re-braid their hair before we leave next week.* "Ribbons or beads on your braids for the wedding?"

"Beads. Lots of beads."

"For both of you?"

Jacquelyn reached over to touch her sister's hair. "Do you want beads Janise, like me?"

"Yes, beads!"

"Well, beads you will both have."

I made a mental note to check to make sure we had beads in the colors that match their dresses. If not, I would grab some this week. One thing for sure, next weekend, we will have a hair braiding weekend.

We finished our nightly ritual of bedtime snuggles and storybooks then goodnight kisses. Lights out.

Still no Matt.

I tidied up a bit, possibly wasting time while I waited up for Matt. I made my way to the shower. *We used to shower together. When did we stop? Does it even matter at this point? Blah, none of that!* I watched some TV, but I can't remember what. However, I do remember turning it off and going to bed. *Did I leave the porch light on?* I convinced myself that it didn't matter. He would come through the garage anyhow.

I was awakened by the grinding of the gears of the garage door. I rolled over and looked at the clock. 2.37AM. With my back turned to his side of the bed, I feigned sleep. As I lay there, I thought about how excited I was about our dresses. Though, not anymore. He'd have to wait. I don't even want to talk to him.

He stopped in the kitchen before coming into our bedroom. I could tell when he entered because the air changed. It was like the freshness disappeared. He walked in, fumbled with his drawers. He found whatever he was looking for and went straight into the bathroom. I didn't move. I listened to him the shower for roughly 10 minutes. Water off. He dried himself. He brushed his teeth. A couple of minutes passed before I felt the weight of him on the bed. I still didn't move.

"Jo?"

Silence. *Should I answer?*

He nudged me. "Jo?"

"Yes?" I was waiting for some excuse or explanation.

"Did you find dresses for the wedding?"

Seriously, that was his question? I was pissed! My body started to heat up. I had a million things to say, but all I could manage was, "Yeah."

SILENT TREATMENT

I decided that I would interact with Matt very little over the next few days. I recognized that he was excited, and his behavior was a tad bit extreme. Now, don't get me wrong. He was usually distracted and disconnected from us, but this right here was on a different level. So, that's exactly what I did. I avoided interactions with him.

If he asked me a question, my answers were short. If the girls were chatting him up or trying to play with him, I redirected. I had stuff to do; therefore, I stayed focused on the tasks at hand. What's funny is... I don't even think he noticed. Hell, for all I know we were both giving each other the silent treatment.

The days flew by. You know how it is when you are looking forward to a getaway. Though, I do love weddings. I was becoming less and less concerned about the wedding and more excited about seeing Miami. I had already figured that Matt would ditch us ASAP. Well, I didn't know for sure but I sure was was hopeful 'cause then we could do the things we wanted to do.

This would be the girl's first wedding. We read books about weddings and looked at pictures. I especially wanted to set some parameters for Jacquelyn for wedding etiquette. As for Janise, I would deal with her cause she was a young toddler. However, for Jacquelyn, expectations were set. She was old enough to learn right from wrong.

The wedding was scheduled for 1:00 in the afternoon, that meant they would probably have a buffet luncheon at the reception. We talked about dress length and place settings and indoor voices. You name it, we covered it. She was allowed to pack toys in her purse. I'd have some emergency supplies in Janise's bag, but those weren't any of her business. With two kids, I know how important it is to keep an emergency stash.

We packed our swimsuits because there was a pool at the hotel, and, of course, the giant bathtub in the suite. We were going to have a good time. I planned on it!

By Tuesday, I had to talk to Matt.

"Matt, just confirming that we are leaving by noon, correct?

"Why noon?"

"Well, that's what you said when decided to leave on Thursday. Besides, check-in is at four. It'll take us about five and half hours to get there including time for a couple of stops."

"I think I said closer to two."

"But you didn't. We were going to scoop the girls on our way out. Humor me, why two?"

"Oh, well Scottie can't leave until two. What's the problem with picking the girls up later?"

I was stunned. "What? Later? Scottie? I thought everyone was arriving on Friday. Is he riding with us?"

"No, but he wants to trail us. His girlfriend is flying into Miami on Thursday night. She won't get there until about 8:00 or 8:30."

My thoughts were running rampant. *I don't care. What does this have to do with us? Why are you planning for us based on someone else? Why didn't you tell me this already?* I took a deep breath. "I'll pick up the girls. You can just ride down with Scottie."

I was being facetious but the expression on his face reflected the wheels turning in his brain. He took a moment to respond. "Are you sure?"

I threw my hands up and laughed as I left the room. *Fuck it. Fuck him.* I was barely out the room before I heard him dialing the phone. He was calling to Scottie to inform him of his change in plans. I could hear him on the phone all excited and shit. *Whatever, it's not like the girls and I haven't traveled alone before. It's what we do.* For a split second, I thought we should just stay home. Hell Matt wouldn't even notice. He would be free to hang with his boys and do what they do.

But two things happened, as I listened to him laugh and joke on the phone: one, I realized that he never laughs and talks with us like that. And two, I deserve a fucking vacation. We were going to Miami, whether he was with us or not!

Eventually, Matt came into the bedroom. With the girl's hair finally braided and beaded, I could begin to pack. He was talking like we were in mid conversation. "Scottie said it was cool for me to ride down with him."

"You don't say?"

"Yeah, I'm glad that he won't be riding alone."

"Aha, good looking out for your boy."

He was completely ignoring my tone and phrases laced in sarcasm or it just didn't matter. He was just happy to get what he wanted.

"Look, Jo, I heard what you said. This shit aint cool. This weekend is so important to me, it could lead to amazing career opportunities. You don't know how important it is for my family to be there with me."

With my back to him, I mumbled. "More important than it is for us to be with you any other time, obviously."

"Did you say something?"

"Nope."

"I am not arguing with you Jo. This wedding is going to be amazing. I told you they are going all out for it. No expense will be spared."

I stopped and looked at him. I was dumbfounded. He nickeled, dimed, and rushed our wedding but is brimming with excitement for this 'no expense will be spared' event. "Amazing."

As he left the room, I heard him say, "Yeah, amazing!"

Let me call in the morning to upgrade our room. I know that I reserved a suite, but I wonder if there's one with a better view or penthouse. If I'm gonna be putting up with this bullshit, I need to make sure I'm having a good, wait a minute, *a great fucking time.*

MIAMI BOUND

Finally, with the car all packed and a quick call to the hotel, it was time to hit the road. At 11:00AM, I picked up my purse and keys on my way to the garage. for the door. Matt met me in the kitchen at the door. "I thought you were leaving at noon."

"Well, I was but since it's just me and the girls, I figured we could head out a little earlier. That'll give us a little extra time to play once we arrive." That wasn't entirely true. I wanted to stop by the grocery store to grab some snacks and a couple or three bottles of wine for the hotel room.

"Oh, I wish you would've told me."

"Is that so? Why?"

"I wanted you to drop me off at Scottie's on your way out."

"Well, come on."

"I haven't finished packing yet and he won't be home until about 12:30."

I laughed, "Are you serious?"

"Yeah, I am."

"Oh well, this train is leaving the station. Why don't you just drive over there?"

"I wanted to leave my car in the garage."

"Just leave it at his house. You guys are coming back, aren't you?" I looked at my watch.

"His girl is riding back with him. I was going to ride back with y'all."

"Whew! Seems like you are making plans with the wrong people."

"What do you mean by that?"

"Nothing. You guys will figure it out." I walked through the door into the garage. Matt just stood in the doorway with this incredulous look upon his face. I proceeded to get in the van, pressed the remote to open the garage, fastened my seatbelt and backed out into the driveway. As the garage door closed, I could still see him standing there. I'm sure he thought I was going to wait for him. I'm usually so fucking accommodating but for this bullshit right here, right now... I was over it!

First stop, gas. Second stop, market. I took my time while gathering snacks, supplies and wine for the hotel. I was in no hurry.

As planned, I scooped Jacquelyn from school then Janise from the babysitter. I had both my map and mobile phone, fully charged, in the passenger seat. We were going on a road trip to Miami. We will be just fine.

With a couple of stops along the way, we arrived at the hotel right at 6:00PM. It took longer than I expected. For one, I had never driven on the turnpike, and two that traffic from West Palm Beach to Ft. Lauderdale was bananas. Next time, if there's a next time, we will leave earlier. Though, I'm not complaining. I have to admit the girls were more patient than me. I was just ready to get there.

Now to the good part, the hotel was nice, really nice! It was the couple's preferred hotel for out-of-town guest. As far as I know, there weren't any events taking place here. But hell, from what little Matt has shared, there could be.

I could tell we were near the coast as we drove. Like to my left, the sky was magnificent and there wasn't a looming skyline on either side. I wondered how close we were to the beach. The sun and palm trees were plentiful, and the wooded areas were lush and thick... very tropical. The hotel entrance was breath-taking with greenery manicured to perfection. Nice.

Once we exited the car, I swear I could smell the saltwater hanging in the air. I debated whether I should put Janise in her stroller or not. I chose not and I'm glad that I didn't. As soon as we entered the hotel, there was a grand fountain centerstage on display in the foyer.

"Coins, Mommy, coins!" Jacquelyn shrieked.

I swear everyone turned to look at us. "Just a moment princess. We need to check in first."

She looked at me, eagerly, as I guided us all to the counter. Jacquelyn held Janise's hand like she needed something to hold on to. Patiently, they waited.

"Hi, we are checking in, last name Monroe."

"First name?"

"Jo. Johanna."

"I have you right here. You are here for the Stansfield Wedding, correct?"

"Yes."

"There was a recent change to your accommodations. Your reservation is no longer near the other wedding guests."

"Yes, that's fine. I made the change this morning."

"Perfect. I need your ID and credit card."

I handed her both. *No longer with the wedding party, hallelujah!* I peeked at the girls, just a couple of more minutes.

The agent completed our reservation, explained a few of the amenities and passed the key cards across the counter.

"Can I leave a key here for my husband? He will arrive later this evening."

"Yes, that's fine. His name?"

"Matt Monroe."

"Ok. Will there be anything else?"

"Would you, by chance, have change for one dollar? It's for the fountain." Jacquelyn hugged me close with her free arm. I smiled at her. "I've got you princess."

"Of course, I have change."

"Thank you."

Change in hand, we headed to the fountain. During our fountain play, I noticed a man looking our way. I couldn't help but notice how handsome he was. His skin was smooth and silky like caramel. When I noticed that he was looking at me, I turned my head. *Was I staring? How rude.* Eventually, I looked in his direction again. He was gone. Relief washed over me. We spent our first 30 minutes at the fountain. The girls were making wishes and enjoying the occasional splash of water. While I, on the other hand, was people watching or moreso, watching a person.

"Want to go to the room or to get our bags out of the car?" I was asking more for myself, but Jacquelyn answered.

"Bathing suit!"

"I agree."

We walked over to the concierge. "Excuse me. I'm in need of a luggage cart, please. Do you know where I can find one?"

"Your name, please?"

"Monroe, Johanna."

"Pleasure to have you stay with us Mrs. Monroe. Did you park in the guest lot?"

"No, I pulled up to the roundabout."

"Perfect. We will bring you bags up and valet will park you."

"Seriously?"

"Yes, I'll follow you to your car."

We led the concierge to our van. He grabbed a cart. We watched him transfer the bags from the van to the cart. Once that was finished, someone handed me a ticket. We continued to stand there while the van was driven away.

"Mrs. Monroe?"

Startled, I replied, "Yes."

"I'll meet you at your suite with your luggage and, uh, things." Note to self, do not bring grocery bags full of wine the next time I stay at this hotel.

"See you there. Thank you."

We entered the hotel in search of the elevator. Once in the elevator, "Jacquelyn will you select twenty-seven? Do you know two? Seven?"

She looked at the panel of numbers but couldn't decide. "Look for the number two then the number seven. They are together." Finally, she moved to select 27. "That's awesome. Way to go!" Off we went soaring into the sky. Janise held on tight. I looked at her little face. She was way too big for a snugly and had almost outgrown her stroller, I guess it's time for her to start holding her own. *Wow, where has the time gone?* The elevator stopped with a ding.

"Alrighty, girls, this is our floor. Let's see..." I was reading the signs as we exited. "We need to go to the right." Jacquelyn looked at me, I pointed. "This way." We passed a few doors until we got to ours on the right, 2706. I used the key card to unlock the door. We pushed the door open and... *oh my everlasting God!* We entered the room; I vaguely remember the door closing behind us. Directly on the other side of the suite was floor to ceiling windows with blue skies and even bluer water as far as the eye could see. We stood silent taking in the view, until there was a knock at the door. I looked at my watch. Surely, it wasn't Matt.

"Yes?"

"I have your luggage."

"Oh yes." I opened the door. "I had forgotten that quickly."

"The view is spectacular, yes?"

"Absolutely!"

I moved from the doorway so he could enter. I grabbed my purse. The girls continued to look out the windows. I removed some cash.

"Thank you." I placed the tip in his hand.

"It is my pleasure. Should you need anything else please do not hesitate to call."

"I won't."

The door closed. Time to explore. *Matt is gonna have a fit.* Listen, I know I said that I was not going to be stuck up in a hotel all weekend, but I take it back. I have no problem being held hostage here. Wow, wow, wow!

"Who wants to go for a quick swim before dinner?"

"Me!"

"Me!"

"Well, let's get into our swimsuits and go!"

We all loved to swim. Both Jacquelyn and Janise had taken lessons. It was a requirement of our pediatrician. "No child should grow up in Florida and not know how to swim." It was offered as a part of his services. Oh, let's not forget that his "parents must be CPR certified annually." He really prepared us for the unthinkable. Watching these two get dressed for the pool, you'd be right to think they've been doing it their whole lives.

The pool had waterfalls and rocked walls and bridges and secluded alcoves. Water was flowing all around us. There were several tiki bars and towel stations. Chaise lounges and tables as far as my eyes could see. Music streamed from speakers hidden in trees. The sun glinted off the water like magic. We found ourselves a section to place our towels and things. The girls took off and jumped right in. Fearless. I wasn't far behind. Even though they both swim well, I keep my eyes peeled for any accidents or issues. I watched jump after jump and heard, "look mommy" so many times, I tried to drown myself in cocktails.

By the time Matt arrived at the hotel, we were having a late dinner poolside. We were talking with another family about how much we loved that the pool was both heated and salt water. My girls were chatting with their kids about this and that and trying to make plans for tomorrow.

I saw his grumpy ass as soon as he entered the pool area. I smiled, "look there's daddy." I hoped that my smile was enough to stop him from being ugly in front of our new friends.

"Hey Daddy!"

"Hey baby."

"Look Daddy, pool."

"I see princess."

As soon as he turned to speak to me, I would've sworn that silence blanketed the pool area. The beat from the music even dropped. "I've been looking all over for you."

"Why?"

He was annoyed. I could hear it in his words. "Have you been to our room?"

"Of course. There's a key for you at the desk."

"I got it."

"Oh good. Have you eaten dinner?"

He barreled right through that question. "They gave us the wrong room."

"No, they didn't."

He started rubbing his fingers together. He was pissed. "We aren't with the wedding party."

"I know."

"What?"

"I called this morning to ask for an upgrade."

"You didn't talk to me about that."

"Did I need to?"

"We need to be near the other wedding guests and events."

"Oh, there are events at the hotel?" He looked away. I knew his ass hadn't shared everything. "You can get another room, Matt."

"This is insane."

"What's the problem?"

"How are you making decisions without consulting me?"

"Easy. You do it all the time. Besides, we'll be spending more time here at the hotel than you. If it's that important for you to stay with the other wedding guests, then just go get another room. You can stay there."

"Where did you park? I need to go somewhere."

"Valet."

"This is ridiculous."

"Ask Scottie for a ride."

He stormed off.

I smiled. I didn't give a damn. We were in paradise and he wouldn't be given the opportunity to ruin this. "Are you guys finished eating? If we wait a bit, we can get back in the pool. Whaddaya say?"

I kept an eye on the door, kinda expecting Matt to come back through it. He didn't but the caramel coated man from the lobby did. I watched him, watch me. He wasn't dressed for the pool. He got a drink and sat a table, just out of distance of the splash zone. He stayed for a few minutes, long enough for him to drink his drink. When I looked over at him, he raised his glass to signal cheers. I nodded my head towards mine and then back in his direction. Cheers.

"Mommy did you see that?"

I turned to get a replay of what I missed. "Wow! That was awesome." When I turned back around in search of him, he was gone.

We stayed and played at the pool until almost 11:00PM. This trip has been in the making for six months. Today, was a long ass day. My babies were exhausted and happy, as was I.

Matt wasn't in the room when we got back. We all took baths in preparation for bed. The girls wanted to sleep in the big room with the big windows. *Why the fuck not?* So, they did. I sat on a chair facing the window and watched the night sky for a while. Visions of the caramel coated man interrupted my thoughts as I gazed longingly at the boats and yachts, sailing and docked. I wondered what it would be like to be on one, lost at the horizon, miles and miles out of reach. The moon beckoned, and stars twinkled. Ironically, the water in the distance looked completely still.

I couldn't wait to take my girls to the beach tomorrow. As I sipped my wine, I decided that we would go right after breakfast. I was so relaxed. I tried to remember a time that I had ever had this feeling of peace. Eventually, and by eventually, I mean after one more glass of wine. I convinced myself to leave my comfy seat. Although, the concierge had already hung the garment bag that contained our perfect dresses. The suitcases continued to stare at me from the floor. *Move your ass, Jo.*

And I'm happy that I did because within minutes exhaustion grabbed a hold of me like a vice grip. Which was probably a good thing because I know in my heart that more bullshit awaits tomorrow. I decided against pouring another glass of wine. I just picked up my glass and swallowed the last little bit. I slipped into bed between my girls. My plan was to watch the twinkling lights from the boats until I fell asleep. That didn't happen, as soon as my head hit the pillow, I was out.

Joycelyn Wells

BULLSHIT IN PARADISE

Death By A Wedding

The sun announced itself. *Damn, I should've closed the blinds before going to bed.* I looked at both Jacquelyn and Janise, unbothered by the radiance. Ha! They were tired. I eased myself out of bed, closed the blinds and went to the bathroom. I watched them from the doorway. *Should I wake them to go potty?* I wasn't ready to wake up yet. They weren't either but they both *needed* to go potty. Though, if one of them had an accident, we would all be awake. No accidents in the big bed. *Please!*

I walked quietly to the bed and whispered to Jacquelyn. "Let's go to potty." She knew the drill. She rolled over and reached for me. I carried her to the bathroom. She never even opened her eyes. Next, Janise's turn. I said, a silent prayer, *"Please oh please don't let her wake up."*

Princess? Time for potty. She didn't move. She's recently potty trained, so we haven't made the night trips too many times. I turned her over and lifted her up. Lifeless. This girl knows how to sleep. We made it to the potty and back to bed, successfully. I went back to turn off the light and wash my hands. Looking in the mirror trying to think of a plan for later, I yawned and came to the conclusion that in this moment, sleep was necessary... the plans would have to wait.

I climbed back into the bed. This time closest to the window because Jacquelyn was holding Janise's hand and in Janise's other hand, she was holding her baby. Now, there's no way, I would interrupt that. With the blinds closed, the room was dark as night. *I needed these drapes in our bedroom at home.* We slept.

Eventually, I awoke to an empty bed, I panicked. *Where was I? Where were the girls?* Immediately, I hopped out of bed. I was hopeful that the girls hadn't awaked Matt. The door to the room was closed. I eased it open and looked into the living room. The girls were sitting in the floor eating dry cereal and playing with their toys.

"Morning little ladies."

"Morning Mommy," Jacquelyn replied.

She always sounds like she's singing when she says, *Morning Mommy.*

"What are you up to Janise?" I said, as I walked closer.

She held up her doll. "Baby."

"Ooohhh I see."

"Did you two get enough sleep?"

"Yes, did you?"

"Well, Jacquelyn, I sure did. Thanks for asking."

"Can we go to the pool today?"

"Hmm, sure, if you like, but I was thinking that we could have a beach day. Janise hasn't been to the beach yet."

"Have I?"

"Yes, but you were about Janise's age when we went. Wait a minute, you mean to tell me that you don't remember?"

She shook her head no.

"Now that's interesting! Well, we will go today, and you will remember, for sure!"

"Yay. Ok." They moved from the floor to the window and begin to point out various things of interest. I heard Janise say, "boat" and "bird."

"Let me check on Daddy to see if he wants to join us." I admonished myself for continuing to try to include him in anything. He wasn't interested. *How many times would he have to tell me 'no' before the message registered for good?* The door was closed to the other bedroom. I'm sure he's pissed that we slept in the other room together but whatever. I knocked. No answer. I turned the knob and cracked the door.

"Matt?"

Still no answer. I pushed the door open.

"Ma...?"

He wasn't even in there. His suitcase was laying on the bed open. So, he had been here at some point. I took a deep breath and closed the door.

"Hey Girls! It's time for breakfast. Who wants pancakes?"

"Waffles!"

"Waffles!"

"And sausage!"

"Well then, waffles and sausage it is! Let's get dressed!"

I noticed Jacquelyn looking around the room. "Princess what are you looking for?"

"My suitcase."

"Oh, I put our clothes away last night. Come in here. I'll show you." They followed me into the bedroom. I pointed out whose clothes were in which drawers.

"Jacquelyn don't forget to put on your swimsuit. You can slip a dress on over it. We are going straight to the beach after breakfast."

"OK, Mommy."

"Come here Janise. I'll help you."

I noticed Jacquelyn looking through her drawer. "What are you looking for Princess?"

"My swimsuit."

"The purple one from last night?"

"Yes."

"It's drying in the bathroom. Remember you wore it to the pool?"

"Yes." She started walking towards the bathroom.

"Princess, it's still wet, so..." I caught myself trying to explain why she needed to wear the dry one. *Does it really matter? What's more important a good disposition or a dry swimsuit that's also gonna be wet and full of sand in little while?* "You know what? I think that's a great idea! Are you tall enough to reach it?"

"Yes, mommy."

"Awesome. Now, what about you Janise? Cold, wet pink swimsuit from last night?"

"Yes."

Jacquelyn giggled, "I'll grab hers, too."

"Excellent."

Once the kids were dressed, I got myself together. *Should I take towels from here? I should've brought some from home.* I decided to grab some from the pool. We can always put them back once we return.

Janise said, "oh my mommy, pretty!" I modeled a bit for her. Jacquelyn joined us. We all began to walk through the penthouse striking poses and pretending to take pictures. Jacquelyn says, "I want to wear my new swimsuit."

I stopped in mid stride, "girl, please, it's time ta go!"

"But mommy this one is cold and wet."

"It sure is but... it's what you chose. So, L E T S G O... let's go!"

They both started singing our morning motivation. L E T S G O... let's go! By the time the elevator got us to the first floor, the conversation had changed.

First stop, concierge. "Good morning, Mrs. Monroe."

I was taken a back. *How did he know my name?* "Good morning," I looked at his name bag, "Javier. It's Johanna."

With a smile, "Ok Johanna." He shifted his attention to the girls. "To what do I owe the pleasure of your visit?"

Janise replied first, "Fountain!"

Then Jacquelyn, "Coins. Do you have coins for the fountain?"

Digging in my bag, I responded before the concierge, "I have coins." I handed Jacquelyn my coin purse. "Make sure you bring this back and don't spend it all in one fountain!"

Javier joined me in laughter as the girls took off to the fountain.

"I guess we have to feed the beast every time we come to the first floor!'

"Seems that way with most of our younger guests. How may I help you?"

"Towels. We are headed to the beach after breakfast. Do you know where we can get some beach towels for the day?"

"Towels?" He replied excitedly. "I can get you way more that towels."

"Well, alright then. I'm all ears."

As he began his spiel, I turned slightly so that I could keep an eye on the girls.

"Private beach... Tiki bar... Transportation... Chaise Lounges... Food... Music..."

I was lost in his words until movement on my left side caught my eye. I turned to watch the long, elegant stride of the caramel coated man who, at this point, I surmised either worked here or was a guest. Either way, his shift or stay was a welcome distraction to my vacation. Javier's voice brought me back to reality. "Johanna?"

"uh, yes? Oh, Javier, that sounds amazing but how much? Can I charge it to my room?"

"No."

"No?"

"That's not necessary, it's included because you know me."

"Do I know you?"

"You will by the end of this vacation."

"Get out of here!"

"No ma'am! If I do that, who's going to make you happy?"

"I like that."

We laughed together. "I'll give you an hour for breakfast. Your chariot awaits."

"Wonderful. See you in an hour."

"Ooh and ask for the papaya!"

I approached the girls at the fountain. "Jacquelyn and Janise are y'all ready? I'm big hungry and I have some great news."

Jacquelyn turned to look at me with a sad face. Panic. "What's wrong?" She held up the empty purse. I continued to search her eyes for something. "What? What is it?"

"We put all the coins in the fountain."

I laughed out loud. *Fuck those coins! Javier said he's got us!* That's what my brain said to itself. "It's okay. We can get more for next time. Thank you for holding on to my change purse." I opened my bag; she dropped the empty change purse inside.

"Now, who's hungry?"

Breakfast was delish. We ate on the lanai by the pool. If I'm not mistaken, we were two tables over from our table last night. There was a buffet area set up which seemed to cater to the kids and early risers. I ordered from the menu. *Table service for me! I'm in paradise!*

"Good morning, Mrs. Monroe."

Since, clearly, everyone knows my name around this joint. "Good morning, it's Johanna, will you please call me Johanna?"

"Yes, of course, Johanna." She blushed. There was an accent for sure, I couldn't place it.

"May I get you something to drink?"

I already felt dizzy from the conversation with Javier. "Do you have any breakfast cocktails?"

"Like a mimosa?"

"Maybe, what's a mimosa?"

She began to describe in detail how mimosas are prepared. We add champagne to orange juice and Grand Marnier then it's garnished with fresh fruit. She had me at champagne! Meanwhile, I was captivated by her smooth tan skin and black hair that framed her face. I looked for a name badge. "What's your name?"

She placed her hand where her name badge should be. "Ingrid."

I was caught off guard, "Ingrid?"

She looked at me blankly.

"Ingrid, is your name? Where are you from?" She didn't reply. "I was just asking. It's no worries. I'll have a mimosa or two." I tried to soften the moment. "Girls, orange juice or water?"

Jacquelyn replied, "Mr. Javier said to ask for papay... papapa..."

Ingrid said, "papaya?"

I was stunned. "He said what? Jacquelyn, did you just ask for papaya?"

"Yes, papaya." She said that like she had an attitude. Her facial expression said, you heard me.

I looked to Ingrid. "I guess they'll be having papaya. What is that it?"

"It's a delicious fruit juice. You'll see."

"Looking forward to it."

I had no idea that he said that. Maybe I just didn't hear him. Oh well, one thing for sure, the babies were paying attention.

Papaya must have been some kinda code word because Ingrid re-introduced herself as Lucia and the table service was magical. The girls had mini waffles that they dipped in syrup and plenty of sausage links. The mimosas flowed and I couldn't have asked for a more perfect morning.

At some point, our breakfast came to a screeching halt. Lucia whispered in my ear, questioningly, "Javi says your chariot awaits."

I leaned back to look at her. Her facial expression indicated that she needed an explanation. "We are headed to the beach, Javier arranged transport."

"Oh ok. I'll see you for dinner."

"Of course," I reached in my purse for some cash. "This is for you Lucia. This isn't to share."

She looked surprised.

"I'm still learning but sometimes you have to do something for only you."

She squeezed my hand, "Your chariot awaits."

"Alrighty, my words trailed off. There he was again. Is he following us? I shook my head to dismiss the thoughts. He's not dressed like the other staff. He must be a guest like us. Jacquelyn grabbed my hand. "Mommy?"

"Yes," I replied, not taking my eyes off the gentleman.

"L E T S G O, it's time to go play at the beach."

I smiled and nodded hello. "It sure is princess, it sure is."

We made our obligatory restroom stop then checked in with Javier. "We are ready."

"Perfect." He handed me a bag filled with towels and water, walked us outside to a van with the hotel logo emblazed on its sides and bid us a farewell.

We settled into our seats. I'm not sure how long the ride lasted, maybe 15 to 20 minutes. We were all quiet and we took in the sites. The pastel colors, palm trees and art deco style all demanded our undivided attention. Everything was surreal. It's like I was in the pages of a magazine. I tried to imagine if this is what it felt like to be in a movie or in love, for that matter. The driver eventually stopped in front of a small hut or cabana. *What was this building called?*

"Is this it? Are we here?"

"Jes."

Latin American. He speaks Spanish. It was the first time I could without a doubt identify the accent. Javier. Lucia.

"Thank you."

"Tell heem dat Javier seent you."

"I sure will." I handed him a tip. "Thanks again."

"Waat time?"

"Time?"

"Pik you uh for hotel?"

"Oh." I looked at my watch. "It's noon now. How about 4?"

"Ok, if later, call Javier at the hotel."

"I sure will."

I spent a moment with my thoughts. I'm not sure if his gaze was intended for me or someone else. I felt like he was looking at me. it was for them or for me. One thing I do know, those mimosas were certainly delicious. I needed to get my shit together. *Is this right? Maybe we should've waited for Matt. Hell, where was Matt?* My little voice reminded me to have fun. *Fuck Matt!* We are safe at the beach in fucking Miami. *Cheers Johanna!*

We approached the cabana. *I've decided to go with cabana until I heard something different.* "Hi, I'm Johanna." I started to give extemporaneous details then stopped and blurted out, "Javier sent us."

"Oh yes, Johanna with her chiquitas."

I smiled. In this moment, I loved Javier. He sees us. He plans for us. He prepares for us. I thanked God for Javier.

"Si, mis chiquitas."

"Hablas espanol?"

I laughed, "muy poco."

He laughed and pointed to himself, "speak English, muy poco."

Well, we would just have to figure it out. Carlos led us through the cabana to the beach area. It was breathtaking...white sands, palm trees and very few people.

"Ju want shade or no shade?" He asked while pointing.

"Shade, for sure." I replied pointing to my already brown skin.

"Beautiful you are. Shade it is."

We chose a section that had four lounge chairs just in case Matt or someone else joined us. *Someone like who Johanna? Javier would tell him where we were, right? Should I have left a note?* I placed our bags on top of the empty lounge chair. The girls started to remove their clothes and shoes. "Wait." They stopped and looked at me, as to ask *for what?* It was my fear. Fear of the unknown. "I don't know. Nothing. Go ahead, get undressed. Let's go play!"

As we played in the surf, I sipped sangria and kept an eye out for Matt. For some deep-seated asinine reason, I expected him to come. He would love it here... *Who was I kidding?*

Instead, Carlos approached us, "ju eat conch?"

"Is it like lobster? I don't know. I have never had conch."

"Oh good, come now. You can try it!"

"Uh ok." Hesitantly, I called out to the girls, "Jacquelyn and Janise, come on we are going to try conch."

They followed me out of the water to our section. Carlos said, "when you are ready, we are ready."

As we dried off, there was a guy pulling a cooler through the sand towards us. We watched him until he stopped in front of us.

"Conch?"

"Yes, Carlos arranged it for us."

"Great. You have conch before?"

"No. I have not."

He reached into the cooler, pulled out a huge conch shell and held it within reach of the girls, "what about you two?"

"I want it!"

"I want it!"

Hell, even I wanted it. I had never seen anything like it. "What is a conch?"

"Conch is a mollusk. It lives in this shell until we are ready to eat it."

"Oh my!" I looked at the girls. "Y'all want to taste the conch?"

They both nodded.

"Ok then, let's taste the conch."

Our beach server, moved to the table and began to unpack his offerings. We gathered around. This experience was new to all of us. I'm sure that I was more afraid than Jacquelyn or Janise. But hey what's this gonna hurt...

We were having a great time. Tasting everything and exploring our palates. It's crazy the way the energy changed. I could feel his presence. I looked around and there he was... Matt. He was plodding across the beach in jeans and a t-shirt, looking all Matt-like. I picked up my glass and drained the contents. Here we go, bullshit in paradise. Before I could speak, the girls saw him.

"Daddy!"

"Daddy!"

He feigned a smile and waved.

I continued to watch him walk towards us. I knew that this wouldn't be a good visit. He wasn't here to join us in our beach party. He was here to rain on it.

"Hey babies."

Neither of them moved from their chairs. He held their attention as he approached me.

"Jo, what are you doing here?"

I pointed to Carlos' spread, "well, right now we are having a conch tasting. Would you like to join us?"

"No. I mean what are you doing at the beach? You know we have the rehearsal dinner this evening?"

I thought back over previous conversations. Never ever was a rehearsal dinner mentioned to me. *Did I miss something?* The girls were waiting patiently. Carlos was waiting. The conch salad was waiting. The waves were beckoning.

"This is our beach day. Rehearsal dinner? Why would we attend that?"

"I'm a groomsman, Jo. Use your common sense."

I fucking hated when he said shit like that. "I'm using my common sense. Clearly, you are way more common than me. So tell me, why would I need to attend a rehearsal for a wedding at which I am a guest?"

"You need to be there with me. Didn't I explain that?"

"So, let me get this straight? Us being with you is important but you being with us, is not? Hmm now that's uncommon for sure.

"More sangria, Ms. Johanna?"

"Yes."

"No, she is leaving. Come on girls."

"No daddy, we want to stay."

I was flabbergasted. *This motherfucker!* I looked at my watch. The expressions on their faces pleaded with me silently. We still had an hour and thirty minutes until our beach time ended.

"Matt, we are leaving here at four. We can talk about this then."

"Come to my room when you get back."

"Your room? Meaning the penthouse?"

"No."

I laughed, "I will not."

He stormed off.

"More sangria?"

"Absolutely. Now, what did I miss? What else is there to try?"

So, he did get another room with the wedding party. He's such an ass. For years, I had longed for him to want to be with me.

"Conch salad."

"Oooh yes!"

After our conch fest, we spent the remainder of our time frolicking in the surf. I had way too much sangria, but I was good. More importantly, the girls had a blast. By the time we made it back to the hotel, we were all beat. I handed our bag and towels off to Javier on our way to the elevator. He was with other guests. So, I just mouthed, *thank you* and kept it moving. I was almost too tried to walk, and I didn't want to talk anyway. However, I wasn't too tired to notice the caramel coated guy chatting it up with some other brothers. When he looked our way, I averted my eyes and dashed to the elevator.

While the girls bathed, I ordered some dinner. Hopefully, with our tired bodies and full bellies, we would sleep very well. Since room service would take thirty minutes, I had some time to spare. So, I showered in the other bathroom. Matt's suitcase was gone. *Oh well.*

With baths completed, swimsuits rinsed and hung to dry, we ate dinner on the balcony and watched the ships pass. We watched the sunset in silence, marveling in its wonder and beauty. I swear I could hear the sizzle of the sun's heat as it looked to disappear into the ocean. I smiled to myself. What a wonderful day! We... I mean, I needed more days like this!

Joycelyn Wells

THE WEDDING

Death By A Wedding

Jacquelyn awoke first. Which was fine because I needed to touch up her edges before we left. Hell, after the pool on Thursday and the beach on yesterday, we all needed a little something done to our hair. With the wedding starting at one, I had my alarm set for 7am. I'm sure we'd use every minute of our time getting ready. Of course, I had not talked to Matt, but I figured we would leave the hotel around 11am.

It's funny 'cause he wanted to talk so bad at the beach but didn't dare show his face before he left for the rehearsal and dinner. Matt will be Matt. If it's not happening for, about or to him... he's not interested. *Selfish ass.* Well, I had already made-up mind to go to wedding without him, even if he didn't make an appearance soon. At least he couldn't say I didn't show up for him. I would uphold my end of the bargain.

As I washed, dried and curled my hair, I thought about us. How did we get here? Were we always here? It was sad to express out loud, but I really had a lot of fun without him. Yes, I know, I have been on alert for his bullshit but most of it missed me. Probably because I made plans

86

that kept me out of harm's way. I was proud of myself. I felt good about the whole weekend, so far.

I was putting the finishing touches on my hair when I heard the door to the penthouse open. My heart dropped. I watched my expression change in the mirror then looked at the time. 10:32am. When I looked back into the mirror, Matt was standing there. "Why aren't y'all dressed?"

"Uh, good morning."

"Don't start Jo."

"Would it fucking kill you to say 'good morning' to your own damn wife? The one you are counting on to make you appear human to these insignificant bastards you so desperately want to impress."

He stood there and rolled his eyes like it pained him to say, 'good morning' to me.

"Good morning, Jo. There... you happy?"

"As a matter a fact, I am happy. The happiest I've been in years."

"Why are you so fucking happy?"

"Nothing to worry about. It has nothing to do with you at the moment You are free to move around however you'd like. Aren't you happy Matt?"

"Not right now."

"That's too bad."

"Why   aren't   y'all   dressed?

"Us? Why aren't you dressed? Don't you have a groom to support?"

"My tuxedo is in the closet."

"Oh, well, don't let me hold you up."

I turned from the mirror and walked towards the door. Matt stepped to the side to allow me to pass. He didn't touch me or breath or anything. It was like walking through a vacuum. It was weird but not unfamiliar. It feels like this at home sometimes, too. The difference is I'm usually trying to fix it or begging him to tell me what's wrong. Though, not today, I can finally see that he is the issue.

"Mommy, your hair looks pretty."

"So, does yours. Thank you, princess."

"Janise come here princess, it's time to get dressed."

We moved around the suite like Matt wasn't there. Finally, he made a move to get himself together. Once we were all pressed and dressed, it was time. Matt came out of the room and paused in the doorway. He was patting his pockets checking for his shit.

I stopped myself from asking, "What are you looking for?" Usually, I would've offered to find it, or I already knew what and where it was. Not today, I didn't care. He could and would figure it out.

"Daddy, you ready?"

"In a second, we've gotta stop by my room."

I replied without hesitation, "we will meet you in the lobby."

"It'll just take a minute."

"No. See you in the lobby. I'll have them bring the van around. Plus, I need to replenish Janise's diaper bag." I got his attention and whispered, "games."

"Games?" He said a bit too loudly. "Jo this is a wedding, not romper room."

"The kids are four and two Matt! You think they are just gonna sit through a wedding without needing something extra?"

"Whatever, pack the games, Jo!"

"I wasn't asking permission."

"Come on my little princesses!"

Jacquelyn replied, "chiquitas!"

"Si, mis chiquitas!"

Janise started singing our chant, "L E T S G O... let's go!"

We joined in and started marching towards the door. Matt was in front of us. So, he proceeded to open it, and we walked right through, singing our song. We chanted on the elevator, all the way to Matt's floor. Once he got off, we continued on our way to the lobby.

As soon as the door opened, I handed Jacquelyn my change purse.

"Thank you, Mommy!" She grabbed Janise's hand. "Come on."

Javier wasn't at the concierge desk. Needless to say, I was slightly disappointed, but the show must go on. "Good morning, will you please have valet bring my van around?"

"Of course."

"My name is..."

"I know who you are Johanna with her beautiful girls."

I smiled. Someone thinks that we are worthy. "Thank you."

By the time Matt got downstairs, the van was ready, the girls had made plenty of wishes; Yet for me, there was only one. My wish... *I love the way I'm feeling, can I please keep it?*

"This way Ms. Johanna." The valet attendant directed as he opened the doors on the passenger side. Janise got in first and climbed into her car seat then Jacquelyn hopped in and sat in her booster. Before the attendant walked away, he said, "You ladies look absolutely beautiful. Enjoy the wedding."

"Thank you so much. We will."

Matt didn't say anything about our dresses. He didn't even tell the girls that they looked pretty in their perfect dresses. I looked at Matt to see if he would secure Janise's seatbelt. Uh he did not. Lord. He just got in the car like he was the only person alive. I walked around the car to fasten Janise's seatbelt.

Matt said, "Hurry Jo, we are running late."

I laughed and replied, sarcastically, "If anyone is late, it's you. We don't have anywhere to be until one."

Once I got in, I asked, "Jacquelyn, were you able to buckle?"

"Yes, Mommy."

"Great. It's time to go. Ready Matt?"

"Yep, just as soon as Scottie gets down here. We are following them."

"Why don't you ride with him? You said we were running late. Now you want us to sit here in waiting on someone else."

"Well, Jo, he has the directions."

I started laughing uncontrollably. "Did you say he has the directions? Like the location is a secret. Seriously?"

He looked at me with disgust.

"Go, Matt! Damn! I have the directions." I pulled the pages out of the diaper bag.

He waited a couple more minutes then pulled out of the hotel parking lot. No one was talking as we rode. It was silent, other than the whisper of music and me giving random directions. I figure the girls weren't talking because Matt gets so antsy and mean when he was driving. We all know to just sit quietly.

We arrived at the church at 11:45am. There weren't many cars, which wasn't surprising because the wedding wouldn't start for another hour or so. The first car we saw when we pulled into the parking lot belonged to Scottie.

"Isn't that Scottie's car?"

"Yeah, it looks like it."

"Hmph."

Matt rolled his eyes at me.

"Go on in. I'll get the girls together."

He didn't hesitate. I wouldn't be surprised that he would deny having a family if he felt like it benefited him.

I talked with the girls again about the importance of weddings. How we had to use our whisper voices if we had to talk. And the only way they could sit next to each other was if they were quiet and played nice. Otherwise, I'd sit between them. Janise is the only one who can go to sleep, if she's tired. Jacquelyn interjected, "it's because you are still little." We shared a pack of cheese crackers and cleaned our hands.

"Jacquelyn, will you put Janise's baby in the diaper bag please?"

"I already did."

"Thank you, princess. Y'all ready to go inside."

"Yes." Jacquelyn asked, "Are you ready Janise?"

Janise nodded yes. "Janise is ready too."

"Thanks for letting me know."

I reached over, turned the car off and proceeded to get out. I walked around to the driver's side to get Janise. Jacquelyn met me over there. We straightened our perfect dresses and wiped our lips. They looked so beautiful. We looked so beautiful. We must dress up more often. "Can you grab Janise's hand?"

She didn't reply. She just took her hand. I picked up the bag, closed the door and took her other hand. We followed the sidewalk into the church.

It was beautiful. I love churches, especially the older ones. I always imagined someone whittling the wood or making the stain glass by hand. Once inside, people were hustling about finalizing the details... flowers, candles, etc. I picked up a program off a chair as we entered the sanctuary. I'd look at it once we got settled. Before we sat, someone said, "groom's family on the left, bride's family on the right."

"Ok, thank you." We sat mid ways on the left. The girls sat side by side to my left. Hopefully, people will avoid our row all together. I'll keep my fingers crossed for that one. We have 45 more minutes to until the wedding begins. "Do either of you need to potty?" They both shook their heads no. *Right.* "Why don't we try now?"

On our way back to our seats, I noticed that guests were arriving. The bride's side was filling in nicely. She is from Miami, so that's makes sense. As the pews filled and the girls entertained each other, I looked at the program. I hope my eyes weren't deceiving me because it said that two very popular R&B singers would be performing during the ceremony. *Oh my goodness! Matt said that they were well off, but I wasn't expecting this.* This is gonna be amazing! Totally worth all Matt's bullshit. I looked outside from my seat. *What kind of security would they need for this type of wedding?*

By 1:15PM, I was playing with the girls. You know trying to keep them occupied while we waited. It's not uncommon for weddings to be a few minutes late. There are a lot of details of which to tend. Everyone was waiting patiently.

At 1:45PM, movement from the door behind the pulpit caught my attention. I expected it to be the pastor and Adam. *Let's get this party started.* Surprise. Surprise. It was Matt. *Was he coming to check on us?* He slid into the pew next to me. I scooted a bit to make room for him.

"Matt, what's going on? It's almost 2:00."

He leaned closer so he could whisper. My heart starting race. *What the fuck is going on?*

"Alicia isn't here yet."

"What? Is she coming?"

"Yeah, at some point, she's at the hairdresser."

"Are you fucking kidding me?"

"Jo, language." He pointed to remind me that we were in church.

"What about the singers? Are they back there with y'all?"

"What singers?"

I opened my program to show him what I was talking about. He looked from the program to me and back to the program. "Shit, I don't know. Adam hasn't mentioned it." He flipped it over to check the names. I guess trying to make sure it was the correct program.

"Language. Well, how much longer? The girls will be hungry and restless soon."

"I don't know, Jo."

"Someone needs to make an announcement. Look at these people just sitting here waiting."

"Good idea. I'll see if the pastor will do it."

"This is a damned mess."

Matt glared at me as a reminder of my current whereabouts. I mouthed, "I know where the fuck I am." He then returned to the back with the other groomsmen.

Another whole thirty and some odd minutes passed. During which time, I sized up the congregation. *Who were the important people that Matt wanted to impress?* I laughed to myself. *That's no longer an issue. What about Scottie's girlfriend? I bet that's her sitting all alone. What's her name again? If Matt comes out again, I'll ask.*

"Mommy, I'm hungry," Janise whispered.

"Do we have any snacks?" Jacquelyn was always looking for a solution.

The door behind the pulpit opened. I checked my watch, it was 2:30PM. My mind was reeling. *Is the bride, ok? Was there an accident?*

Hell, did she change her mind? Sweet Jesus, please say the bride is here. Maybe that's the pastor or father of the bride, we will all know soon enough. He walked quickly to the microphone. The chosen one. The brave one. Coming to deliver the news... the good, the bad, and/or the ugly.

"Good afternoon, everyone." *He has a lisp.* "You all are looking so beautiful today." *Yeah, and?* We were all sitting at full attention. He paused for a few seconds. I could barely contain myself. *What, Mr.? What's going on?* "I wanted to let you know that the bride..." The whole congregation took a deep breath. *The bride, what?!* He continued, "the bride is running late." We let out a collective groan.

Someone from the front row asked, "she's coming, right?"

We all wanted to hear the answer.

"Yes, she's coming." He looked terrified. He scanned the room before he continued, almost with a whisper, "she's at the beauty shop."

"What?"

"Huh?"

"Did he say..."

Someone completed that question, "beauty shop?"

"Yes, she's under the dryer. These things take time."

He did an about face and dashed through the door. The conversation was on street level now. Everyone forgot that we were in the church. Some people got up to leave. I wanted to know where they were going but how was that my business? Without taking my eyes off the leaving guests, I dug into our bag searching for snacks. Finally, I looked and smiled, the girls were already snacking. I reached out my hand. Hell, I was hungry, too.

The kids noticed the jingling first. Janise grabbed my arm. I looked at her, "yes, princess?"

She pointed outside, "ice cream."

"Yes, sounds like the ice cream truck."

I was having an internal battle with myself. *Wouldn't it be rude to leave a wedding to go outside for ice cream? But what if the wedding hadn't begun yet?* I was processing all that shit, when some grown ass man yelled, "That's the gelato truck. Y'all want something?"

People started laughing like crazy and leaving the church. I looked at the girls, "You heard the man, y'all want something?" Both nodded their heads. "Well, let's go." We scooted out of our pew and left the church along with many others.

Well, the gelato truck doesn't just sell gelato. Did you know that? We brought mangoes, several bags of potato chips, some candy, water, some rum punch and gelato. We walked back into the church with a grocery bag. I held it low to be discreet. But damn, it's our first time in Miami and in this situation, and not to mention, my babies were hungry. So, it was whatever.

An hour later, our announcer friend reappeared. There were less guests of which to be afraid this time around. He was smiling. "The bride is here." We breathed a collective sigh of relief but that was it. Hell, it was 3:30PM. This shindig is two and half hours late. At this point, let's just get this shit over with.

I checked our area soon to make sure that all our treats and trash were stashed away. I told the girls that the wedding would be starting soon.

"I've gotta use the potty."

"Me too."

"Me three. Let's hurry." I took our trash with us.

We returned to our seats. The wedding hadn't started yet. Which was fine, I didn't want to come in late after we'd been here this whole damn time. It dawned on me once we were seated that there weren't any members of the bridal party lined up in the foyer. If the bride is here, shouldn't they be lined up for the processional?

The lighting changed in the church. Everyone looked around. We realized it wasn't the lighting it was the sunlight. The sky had become overcast. *It's going to rain.* There was a flash of lightening and a crash of thunder then... the bottom fell out of the sky. Still patiently waiting until... Boom! Crash! It sounded like the doors of the church had been kicked in. I'm certain that someone, other than me, shouted, "what the fuck?"

We turned to see what was going on. There were groomsmen everywhere, tumbling and falling about trying to get in out of the rain. I couldn't even count them all. They weren't smiling. I locked eyes with Matt. He was dusting raindrops off his tuxedo.

"There's Daddy!"

"Hi Daddy!

He took this opportunity to come sit with us again. I mean how could he ignore those sweet voices in front of all the people he needed to impress.

"Y'all alright?"

"Yes. I thought the bride was here."

"She is. Well, that's what I heard."

I looked at him dubiously, "that's what you heard? Matt, what's going on?"

"I have no idea."

"How's Adam?"

"Patient."

"Where are y'all coming from? Why were y'all all out in the rain?"

"We were told to line up because the bride had arrived. As soon as we did, it started to pour."

He looked defeated, as he sat speechless for a minute or two. I noticed the groomsmen milling about talking to their folks. Scottie was sitting with that young lady. *Ha! I knew that was her.* She should be sitting with us.

I handed Matt a bag of the chips that we scored from the gelato truck. He looked at me questioningly. I shook my head, "don't ask." That response was sufficient. He just sat there, as if reevaluating his whole life, and ate the chips.

Our announcer appeared again at 4:00PM. The whole congregation was over it. If Matt wasn't in the wedding, I'm sure we would've been gone by now.

"As I said earlier, the bride and her bridal party are here. The ceremony will begin momentarily."

"What's momentarily?"

"What's taking so long?"

"15 minutes." "She had to nurse the baby." He lowered his head and hurried off to avoid any more questions.

The whole church erupted in uncontrollable laughter. I'm not sure if we were laughing because it was funny or because there wasn't anything else left to do. People were mocking him, repeating his words with the lisp. *Lord, bless him.* It's not his fault but it was comical.

Matt stood.

"Hey, Matt, before you leave, did you find out anything about the singers?"

He dropped his head and walked off.

I laughed to myself. He was so hyped about this wedding. Pretty much sacrificing everything, including his family, for this moment. He was truly deflated. *Lord, bless him too.*

"Johanna? Johanna?

"Yes?" I turned to face a gentleman. The gentleman from the pool at the hotel. "Yes, I'm Johanna."

"Hmm, I'm Anthony."

He was dressed in a tuxedo similar to Matt's, so I figured out that he was a groomsman. "Hi Anthony."

"Adam wanted me to check with you to see if you had any more chips or snacks of any kind in your bag."

It took my mind a moment to comprehend what he was asking. Matt must have told Adam that I have snacks. "Yes, I have more. What would he like?"

"All of them. He said that he would pay you back."

"Well, ok, um..." I pulled the gelato bag out and handed it to him.

"Thanks. Do you mind if I borrow those?"

I looked down. The Uno cards were visible in our bag. I reached in to retrieve them. "These? Sure. Here you go."

I handed the cards to him. He replied, "you look amazing."

I blushed. I didn't even get a chance to thank him before he dashed off. So, the groom and his men were hungry and bored. *Johanna saves the day.*

Just as I was giving up hope, a young man, possibly early teens, appeared and took his seat in the choir stand next to a portable CD player and a microphone. Now, that's odd. *Was he in charge of the music?* It was 4:30PM. He nodded his head in agreement with someone behind me then pressed play. One full instrumental played before the pastor and Adam entered the sanctuary from the pulpit door and walked to the altar. *Shit!*

It's time! The excited murmurs of the guests filled the church, and someone even clapped. The clapping may have come from me. I'm not admitting or denying it. Just know there was clapping! Anyway, they took their positions. *It's go time, baby!* Ok, so here's an update, the announcer and the minister were not the same person.

I followed along the program because there was supposed to be a live performance during the seating of the parents. The music director changed the CD. It was then I put two and two together. I felt as if I had been bamboozled. The microphone wasn't for a singer, it was placed on the seat by the speakers on the CD player, so that the sound would project louder. And, furthermore, there would not be any performers, that notation on the program just meant that CDs of them singing their songs would be played during the ceremony. *What in the whole mess?*

The parents were seated on their respective sides. *Oh my! The man making the announcements was the bride's father!* Their song played in its entirety. *Why play the whole song? We've wasted enough time already, haven't we?* I watched the music director change the CD. He pressed play.

The doors of the church opened. The wedding processional began. It was apparent that they stayed true to practice 'cause when I tell you they were walking slow... trust that they were. There weren't as many groomsmen as bridesmaids. I flipped the program over to count the bridesmaids. *Twenty fucking two.* Who has twenty fucking two bridesmaids? And that's not including the maid and matron of honor or the flower girls.

The song changed for the entrance of the maid, matron of honor and flower girls. The ring bearer was asleep. *Lucky him.* The song played through. The little music director was changing those CDs ever so quietly. He was taking his job seriously. The doors to the sanctuary closed.

The music director pressed play, yet again. A familiar melody filled the room. Yes, it's about damn time! *Dum, dum, dum, dum, Here Comes the Bride.* My anxiety changed to excitement. The pastor spoke, "Please stand for the bride."

We stood. In that very moment, time ceased to exist. I didn't think about all of the chaos that ensued prior to the start of the wedding. The bride was stunning. Her hair was beautiful, and she was smiling. Adam was handsome and beaming with joy. The looks they shared with each other, assured the whole lot of us that they would wait an eternity, again, for this very moment. Relief washed over me, and I held my girls close, hopeful that they could feel the love in this moment.

Silence filled the church. The music director sat proudly waiting for his next assignment. The pastor asked the obligatory, "Who gives this bride to this man?"

"Her mother and I do, willingly," the well-known voice of her father responded. He sat with his wife. I thought about the anxiety they must have felt throughout the day.

The remainder of the ceremony went off without a hitch. They shared traditional vows of 'love, honor and obey.' They said, "I do." And they exchanged a kiss, so passionate, that I believed the intention of their words.

"Ooohhh!" "Yes!" "Ok then!" "Get a room!" All of which were very appropriate responses from their guests.

The pastor announced, "Please allow me to introduce, after a very long but worthwhile wait I must admit, Mr. & Mrs. Adam & Alicia Stansfield. We all laughed, cheered and clapped. The music director nodded to whoever then pressed play. The bridal party danced their way up out of there! The bride and groom followed. Before they could get out the sanctuary good, guests were peeling out of the parking lot.

The girls and I moved around a little. We waited for Matt to finish up with wedding photos. We visited the restroom again. We smelled the flowers. We danced a little. We even practiced walking down the aisle until the wedding party came in.

"There's daddy!"

"Yes, it sure is. He has to take some more pictures before we leave."

We watched and continued to wait, patiently.

"You two know what?" I smiled at them.

"What?" "What Mommy what?"

"I am so proud of you both. You were such big girls today! How old are y'all? Like 6 or 7?"

"No," with giggles. "I'm four and she's two."

"There's no way! You must both be in big kid school already."

"Not yet!"

I started to tickle them and give kisses. They squealed with joy. We are having so much fun on this trip, minus this crazy ass wedding but it's ok. We made it through and now it's almost time for the reception. Party time!

Matt came over when then finished. "Y'all ready?"

"Absolutely!"

"Anybody gotta potty?"

Janise thought about it. Jacquelyn replied, "no."

"Ok, then, Janise let's give it a try."

"I'll come too," said Jacquelyn.

Matt grabbed my arm. "Johanna, why didn't you take them already?"

I looked at him with an expression that said, 'muthafucker take your hand off of me!' He read it right too because he let go.

"I'll be waiting in the car."

We kept on walking. I had to get myself together in that bathroom. We been up in this bitch all fucking day waiting on this wedding to take place and now he wants to question my timing on some shit. I was just staring into the mirror trying to calm myself.

Jacquelyn touched my arm, "Mommy you ready now?" I snapped out of whatever it was that held me still. I look from Jacquelyn to Janise then back at my reflection.

Their little faces reminded me of the reason why I chose happiness this weekend, for us. I chose it for us. "Yes, princess, I am."

Come on, "It's time for the reception! Are y'all ready to dance the night away?"

Matt was standing outside of the bathroom when we exited. He looked at me. I looked at him. "What? I thought you were waiting in the car?"

"How can I if you have the keys?"

"Where are your keys?

"I didn't bring them."

"Oh." "Let's go ladies."

I unlocked the doors and handed the keys to Matt. I got in from the side door with the girls.

Matt said, "You ridin' in the back now?"

"What difference does it make?" *Why the hell was he asking? It shouldn't matter to him.* Actually, the rain had started again. I wasn't trying to get wet. So, I entered through the back just so I could get the girls situated then I'd climb through.

"Oh, ok. Now here you go."

"You need directions or are you following someone?

"I see you got jokes."

"Well, which it is?" One of the members of the wedding party flashed their lights at Matt, so he could pull out. "Looks like someone decided for you." *Following.*

THE RECEPTION

"Matt, this is a funeral home. Are sure this is the right place?"

"Everybody came here Johanna."

"Let's just wait until the bride and groom get here before we go in."

Scottie parked next to us, but it was raining so hard we could barely see him. Matt tried to motion for him to let down his window. He didn't respond. So, Matt lowered his window. Scottie's girlfriend did the same.

"Is this the right place?"

Scottie replied, "Yeah man, I believe so. We all followed the best man."

"Reggie. Well, this is weird as fuck."

"Matt, tell Scottie's girlfriend to get in the van with us, while y'all go check everything out." I looked at the clock on the dash, 6:02PM. *Wow!*

"Shante? Johanna asked if you'd like to get in the van with them, while we go check everything out."

"Yes, here I come."

"Hurry, close the window, Matt. There's an umbrella in the backseat. Jacquelyn, can you pass daddy the umbrella?

She handed towards the front. I took it and gave it to Matt.

"Be careful out there, I bet it's slick as hell."

Matt got out the car. The umbrella didn't protect him from this torrential downpour. As soon as he let that bitch up, the force of the wind inverted it. It was quite funny to watch. I knew one thing; I didn't care if this was the right place or not. I'm not getting out.

Shante opened the door and hopped in.

"Dammit man!"

We both started laughing. I opened the glove box to get her some napkins. "Here you go love. I'm Johanna."

"Hey girl, I'm Shante. This rain is crazy."

"That's the exact word that Jacquelyn used to describe it too! Crazy as hell!"

"Is it a hurricane or something?" Shante asked.

"Nah, it's not quite hurricane season yet. It seems like there would've been an announcement about a weather system on the news or the radio.

"We haven't watched the news or listened to the radio all weekend long."

"Neither have we."

"When is hurricane season?"

"June through November," I replied.

"Well, whatever it is, I don't like it."

I laughed, "me either. Shante let me introduce you to my daughters, Jacquelyn, and Janise."

"Hi girls." "Thanks for letting me wait with y'all."

"I wish we would've met sooner. I saw you at the church, but I didn't know at the time that you were Scottie's girlfriend."

She held her hand out, "Fiancé, we got engaged on Thursday evening!"

"How wonderful! Love all around us."

We stopped talking when a limo pulled up. Or was that a hearse? Either would have been appropriate for this moment. Fortunately, the rain was easing up. I don't think that I took one breath the whole time I watched the car. I wanted to see who got out. The driver stopped under the overhang, got out, walked around the car and opened the door. Adam stepped out and reached in for Alicia. I screamed, "no fucking way!"

Alicia and I said at the same time, "the reception IS here, at a funeral home."

Scottie came to get Shante. She waved goodbye and said, "see you inside."

It sounded like a question to me. "Yes, inside." Matt would literally have to come get us. We can wait right here all night if need be.

Here comes Matt. *Dammit man.* He gets in the van and slams the door. "I threw that cheap ass umbrella away."

"Of all the bullshit that has happened today, that's what has you in an uproar." Seriously, I can't make this shit up. I laughed.

"What's funny, Johanna? I'm wet as hell."

"Yes, you and all of Miami."

He sat there fuming. "Look, are y'all coming in or not?"

"Oh, we have a choice?"

"Johanna, you are being really extra this weekend. No there isn't a choice."

"Then why ask?"

"Just come on. Adam & Alicia are already here."

"Yes, we saw them when they arrived. I thought it was a hearse."

"You've got more jokes."

Some man in a tux came running out of the funeral home across the parking lot. I was pointing and asking who he was, when he bust his ass on the pavement. "Oh my god, Matt. Did you see that? Who was that?"

"Damn! Oh, he got up, he's ok."

Whew child.

I climbed through the van to get the girls unbuckled and ready to go inside. Janise was hanging tough on this trip. She's gonna sleep like a log tonight.

"Before we go inside, I need for you both to know that this is a scared space. There's won't be any running or playing or loud talking. We will find us a seat for dinner."

Jacquelyn asked, "no dancing either, Mommy?"

"Princess, I have no idea. We will have to see once we get inside."

"Matt, will you carry Jacquelyn? I've got Janise."

Before he could respond, Jacquelyn said, "I can walk Mommy."

"Well, alright big girl, let's walk then. We have to be very careful." I was holding Janise until she started trying to get down. "Oh ok, you too, huh?" I left the bag in the car but put the key fob in my bra. There was no way we would get stuck here for too long, waiting on Matt's ass.

As a family, we entered the *Reflections Cremations Services and Funeral Home.* The invitation specifically stated, 'Reception Immediately following at the Reflections Event Hall'. Well, here we are. People were seated in chairs and clustered in groups crying and talking quietly on the right, clearly in mourning. The sign by the door read, Viewing Service of Roberta Smith, May 23rd, 6:00PM.

I tugged on Matt's arm. He looked and kept walking. Across the room on the left side, there was a small table with two chairs. Matt motioned for us to sit there. Instead of replying, *seriously?* I asked, "where is the bathroom?"

"If you don't sit now, we may lose these seats to someone else."

"Are you serious?"

He glared at me. "You hold the seats. We are going to the bathroom."

As we walked through the funeral home, we looked into a room with an open casket. Family members and friends were gathered around. I tried to read the sign to see who was being mourned but there was someone standing in front of it. It was clearly not the same family and friends of Roberta Smith. I was completely outside of myself. *Now, this is crazy.* Shante was in the bathroom sitting on a sofa. We startled her.

"Hey Johanna."

"Hey Shante. What are you doing in here?"

"Honestly?"

"Of course, honestly."

"I'm hiding out."

I laughed. "I don't blame you. What in the hell is going on out there?" "Jacquelyn, can you help Janise use the restroom?"

"Yes, Mommy."

"Thank you."

Shante replied, "Too much. So, according to Scottie, there are two viewings going on. And because the wedding is so late, the reception overlapped the viewings."

"Uh Shante, riddle me this, why is the reception at the funeral home in the first place?"

"Alicia is studying to be a mortician. She works here and thought it would be a great place for the reception."

My eyes widened. "No way!"

"Yep!"

We sat there silent until the girls came out of the stall. I spoke first, "I'm thinking we will get a quick bite to eat then go back to the hotel. I am famished."

"Where are you going to eat?"

Surprised, I asked, "What? Isn't there food here?"

She just looked away then back at me.

"Shut the front door! There isn't any food?"

"Well, Adam told the groomsmen that the caterer told him that 'she didn't come because it was storming so bad all afternoon and she didn't know if they were still going through with it'."

I was dumbfounded. "What? Are you serious?"

"Girl this is a comedy of errors. The whole damn day. If there isn't any food, we are leaving. We are hungry. Hell, we gave our snack stash to the groomsmen at church."

"Oh, they got the mangos from you?"

"Uh yes, now I need them back."

Shante laughed and asked, "can I leave with y'all?"

"Yes ma'am. I'm sure we won't be much longer. I won't leave without you."

Matt was still holding our seats down. When we approached, he and Anthony both got up. *Whoa!* "Hello gentlemen, no need to get up. We are going to the event hall. Isn't it time for dinner?" I had to act like I didn't just spend 10 minutes getting information from Shante. Matt's ass ought to be ashamed of himself acting like all this shit is normal.

Anthony spoke before Matt, "Well, hello beautiful."

I smiled and replied, "Why thank you, such a nice compliment."

"Johanna, right?"

Matt was just standing there.

"Right."

Anthony began introductions, "this my good friend Matt."

Matt and I spoke at the same time. I said, "good friend, huh?"

While Matt replied, "Man, why are you introducing me? I know her."

Anthony looked back and forth between the two of us. "Oh, you do?"

"Yes, she is my wife."

Awkward. I smiled dumbfounded. *How does he not know that Matt has a wife?* He introduced him as his 'good friend.'

"Well, as I was saying, we are ready to go to the event hall to get something to eat." I had to break the tension.

Anthony spoke nervously, "I wish there was some food here. I'm so hungry my stomach is eating itself." We laughed uneasily.

"You mean to tell me that there isn't any reception food? Both Matt and Anthony just looked at me. Neither of them wanted to tell me the news. But I knew already. *Ain't this some bullshit.* Upon realizing that this was some bullshit, Anthony excused himself.

"Jo, how do you know him?"

"I don't. Look, Matt, we need to get something to eat. It's been a long day for all of us. This isn't fair to the girls." Looking around, they appeared to be the only kids there... "to our kids."

"It should only be a few more minutes."

I looked at my watch. 6:57PM.

"Reggie went to get some chicken, sides and biscuits from a local chicken restuarant. He should be back soon."

I searched Matt's face to see if he were truly ok with this mess. He was.

"Matt, you do whatever you want. I've had enough for today. I am not going to sit up anywhere else any while longer. The girls and I are leaving. You can catch a ride back to the hotel with someone else, can't you?"

I started to walk off then remembered that he wanted me to meet some important people that may lead to a great opportunity. I stopped and turned to face him. "Oh, I nearly forgot, who are the people you wanted us to meet? Can you introduce us now?"

"I'll walk y'all to the car."

On the way out, I motioned to Shante that we were headed to the car. She nodded and held up a finger, letting me know that she'd be just a minute longer.

The rain had stopped and now it was sweltering hot once again. "Matt, did you change your mind about us meeting those people? You literally stressed how important it was for them to meet your family. So, what happened?"

Whatever he was about to say, he didn't want to say it. I waited. He needed to say something. He waved at Reggie as he pulled into the parking lot them mumbled something incoherent under his breath.

"What? What did you say?" I leaned in.

"They left already."

"Oh wow. How did we miss them?"

"They left before the wedding even started. They had to catch a flight."

"Are you serious?" I could not hold my laughter. "Boy you are as big of a disaster as this whole damn day."

"Whatever Jo. Don't think you aren't gonna tell me how you know Anthony. We are gonna talk about it as soon as I get back to the hotel." He turned and walked back inside, passing Shante and someone else along the way.

I didn't even respond to that stupidity. "Hi ladies, going my way?"

Shante made introductions. "Thanks Johanna so much for taking me back to the hotel. This is Reggie's girlfriend Cheryl. Do you mind if she rides back with us?"

"Not at all. Hi Cheryl. You'll have to climb to the back row. Is that ok?"

"Yep, that's fine. I'll ride in the trunk to get away from here."

We all died laughing. "I know that's right!"

"Jacquelyn and Janise say hi to Ms. Cheryl."

"Hi." "Hi."

"Y'all all buckled in?" Everyone responded yes. "Good, now let's go get something to eat."

I handed Shante the map. "Here you are, get us back."

She laughed, "uh ok."

Cheryl chimed in, "I know where we are going. I live here. We are just staying at the hotel because Reggie wanted to be with the other groomsmen."

"Well, well, well, I feel better already."

We decided that they would come to my suite, and we'd order room service. However, we did stop for wine and vodka. We pulled to valet and started unloading. "Mrs. Johanna and her beautiful daughters. So good to you."

"Well, thank you. It is good to be seen."

Once inside the lobby, I remembered that I forgot to get coins for the fountain. "Shit!"

Jacquelyn asked, "what's wrong mommy?"

"I forgot to get coins for the fountain."

"It's ok. We can make a wish tomorrow."

"We sure can. Did your wish come true today?"

"Not yet, I wished that we could go swimming."

I replied, "this weather has been crazy today. What about swimming in the giant tub in the penthouse? Does that count?"

"Can we wear our swimsuits?"

"Absolutely, whichever one you want."

"Mommy?"

"Yes princess? Did your wish come true?"

"I do believe so. I'm getting closer to happiness with every minute that passes!"

Javier, "Ms. Johanna and the chiquitas!"

We waved at Javier and went on the elevator.

Shante asked, do you stay here all the time? How does everyone know you?"

"Nope, it's my first time. I wondered the same time. Which floor?"

"Tenth," said Cheryl.

"Same here," added Shante. "I believe your room is right across from ours."

Jacquelyn selected the 27th floor. "Matt's room may be across from yours. The girls and I are in 2706. Get changed and come on up. I'll order some food."

"Ok, see you soon."

"Me too?" asked Cheryl.

"Yes, of course."

.

MY REFLECTION

As promised, the first thing that I did was to order food. Because we were starving and the ladies would be joining us, I ordered several menu items. We could mix and match and share. If someone wanted something different, they could always place another order.

I undressed myself then helped the girls. My feet hurt. I was tired. I was slightly irritated, but I refused to give in to any of it. I couldn't push Matt's behavior out of my mind. He was unbelievable. How could he spend a whole weekend with folks, and they didn't know that he was married? Did he even tell anyone that his family was here? Yes, I know it was my decision to get a different room. We needed more than a room with two double beds. Our family needed more. We deserve more. It's not like we stayed at another hotel. We were right here! And, if he were going to act like we didn't exist, why did he ask us to come?

Even at the church when Anthony asked me for snacks, it's because Adam asked him to. Not Matt. So, how did Adam know that I had snacks? Did Matt tell him? Or was it because he assumed I would because the kids were with me? What's even weirder is that at the time Anthony asked, he didn't know who I was, but he had to have recognized me from the pool. Maybe that's why he volunteered to come over. Was Adam just like go ask that lady if she has some snacks? Why didn't Matt come get the snacks? So many questions...

I figured the only reason Shante knew who we were was because Scottie would've told her. He seems to be generous and forthcoming with the information. She knew about the food and even the reasoning behind holding the repast, I mean reception at the funeral home. She was in the know. I couldn't wait for her to get up here to share some more details.

It was going to take forever to fill this bathtub. It was huge. Well, better start now. Maybe there will be enough water in the tub for a mini swim, after the girls eat some dinner. Room service usually takes about thirty minutes. Yeah, that should be plenty of time. I know Janise must be tired, she's been up all day. I guess all the excitement had her attention. Well, it had mine too and yet, I can't wait to go to bed.

"Mommy, will you help me?"

I realized that I was standing at the window in my underwear getting lost in this bottomless pit of thoughts and suppositions. "Uh yeah princess. What are you trying to do?"

Jacquelyn held up her swimsuit.

"Oh, now you want to wear the new one. How about that? You won't even get to show it off at the beach."

Janise came in moments later holding hers up. "You need some help too?"

She nodded her head.

"Alrighty, give me just a minute. You'll be next." These girls are my reason. They need me. I need them.

As soon as we got Janise's swimsuit on, there was a knock at the door. "Who could that be?"

The girls giggled.

"What do you guys think? Is it dinner or Ms. Shante and Ms. Cheryl?"

We walked over the door and opened it.

It was Shante and Cheryl. "Hey ladies. You found us. The food will be here soon."

Jacquelyn squealed, "I was right!"

"Yeah, you were! I was hopeful for food."

Shante and Cheryl just stood right inside the door looking around. It took me a second to realize what was happening. They were having the experience that I had when I first entered the penthouse. That overwhelming feeling of awe and excitement. I stepped out of the way and moved a couple of toys to clear a path for them.

Eventually, Shante spoke, "What the fuck, Johanna? The place is like wow... that's all I've got. Just wow. You've been up here this whole time?"

"Well, yes but it's not mine. I just rented it for the weekend. You, too, can rent it and many others just like it." I'm pretty sure I sounded like a game show host. Well, I tried anyway.

Cheryl spoke up, "I drive past this hotel all the time. I had no idea they had rooms like this. Jeez, look at this view."

"Come on in y'all. Make yourselves comfortable. The food will be here soon."

"Y'all want a drink? The wine and vodka are on the bar. Ice is in the fridge."

Cheryl moved first, "I ain't never leaving. Oh yeah, before I forget I left your room number in our room for Reggie so he can call me when he gets back."

Shante said, "oohh I did the same thing."

"That's not a problem."

There was a knock at the door. We all shouted, "FOOD!" When I opened the door the room service attendant was laughing. He must have heard our elation through the door. I grabbed some cash from my purse and thanked him. We organized the food on the table and started to make plates. It was literally a smorgasbord of goodness. The girls sat at the table, while Shante and Cheryl sat on the chairs in the living room.

Before I got too comfortable, I excused myself to check on the bath water. It wasn't full enough yet. I made a mental note to turn it off in just a few more minutes. I chose the seat that would allow me to see into the bathroom, I could watch the girls play and get up to check on them without interrupting the conversation. I copped a squat on the floor by one of the windows.

Shante asked, "Why is Matt staying in a different room?"

I laughed to myself. No wonder she has all the information. She's definitely not afraid to ask the tough questions. *Well, is it really a tough question?*

"Damn Shante, you gonna ask just like that?" Cheryl admonished. "I mean, I was wondering too..." Her voice trailed off.

"It's ok. It's a great question. And I'll answer to the best of my knowledge. Honestly, other than wanting to be near the groomsmen, I don't know. We were traveling with kids, so I thought we needed something bigger. So, I upgraded the room. He chose to get another room." I threw up my hands indicating I don't know. "Hang on a second, let me check on this water. I'll be right back."

"Alright girls your pool bath is almost ready. As soon as you finish eating, you can go play." I settled back on to the floor.

Shante continued to talk. "It's got me worried. Scottie and I just got engaged. I don't know if I would be ok with him staying someplace other than with me."

"Who says that I'm ok with it?"

"You seem like you are."

"I am ok. I'm not ok with my husband treating me like an option but I am ok. Plus, someone has to take care of the kids. If not me then who? Matt's been traipsing around for months like he's the only person to exist. I can't afford to do that. I can't get caught up in his bullshit. The girls are depending on me."

"Mommy we are ready to get in the tub."

"Ok, let me help. Here I come. I'll be right back ladies."

I went into the bathroom, turned the water off and pulled out some bath towels. "Be very careful in here. No jumping in and out. I'll be in the living room. Call me if you need to get out or when you are ready to get out, ok?"

"Ok."

"Ok."

When I reentered the living room, the ladies were quiet. I broke the silence. "Does anyone need a refill or refresher on their cocktail?" Cheryl stood. "I'll top you off. Have a seat."

"If you insist!"

"What about you Shante?"

"Of course, bring it on."

The kids played and we continued to talk about so much relationship shit. I went on to explain that it's not my job to make him love me. It's my job to love myself. What's funny is I didn't realize that I was missing anything until the conversations about Adam's and Alicia's wedding started taking place. Over the years, I had settled into our routine at home. Matt was for Matt. Jo was for Matt. I thought we were happy. If I could keep him happy then I'd be happy. That's what I genuinely thought.

"This trip made me realize that our relationship was truly yucky."

Cheryl laughed, "Damn Jo, yucky."

"Yes, yucky. Look Shante, if you want your relationship with Scottie to be magical then don't settle for anything less, like I did and like I continue to do. Regardless of the reasons. Demand what your heart desires."

"Ok, enough about that. Do y'all mind if we talk about the elephant in the room?" Their eyes widened. "Duh! That wedding!"

We all hesitated. I know my concern was trying not to come across as mean or catty. I took a deep breath and said, "Fuck it, I'll start." Both of their heads snapped and turned in my direction. I mean, seriously, who was going to do something to me, is I talked about it? They were listening intently. I sipped my wine before I uttered a single syllable, "three and a half hours late? Seriously?"

"But the best thing of all is, Adam waited for her to have exactly what she wanted."

"You are so right."

"He was smiling and patient the whole time."

"I love that."

That opened the flood gates. We chatted like old friends in a trusted space about the programs, the number of bridesmaids, the DJ and even the father of the bride. I admitted that I thought the 'performed by' meant that Whitney was going to be there. Silly me. They both laughed for a while about that. Well, until the phone rang. It was my first time hearing the odd noise. It startled me. "I'll be right back." I looked in on the girls along my way.

"Hello." I listened to the baritone voice vibrate through the phone. "Why yes, yes they are here?" Shante and Cheryl looked my way. "Come on up. The door is open. Okay, bye." I hung up the phone and propped the door open. "Your men folks are on the way."

"Ha! They found us!"

"And, trust me, that's a good thing."

As soon as I joined the ladies, we picked up our wedding conversation where we left off. Shante shared her ideas and wants for her wedding.

Cheryl asked something about ending a hoe phase before marriage and we almost died laughing! We didn't even get to address that topic before the door opened.

We collected ourselves as quickly as possible. I waved hi as I went into the bathroom to check on the girls. I yelled to Shante and Cheryl to make sure everybody was comfortable. And that I'll be out in a moment.

I could hear them talking about all the food we had. Someone made a drink. Laughter and oohing and aahing about the view. It was a dope ass view.

The girls were ready to get out of the tub. They were tired as hell. I dried them off and slipped their pjs on. As soon as they were under the cover it was lights out. I went back into the bathroom to tidy up. None of the male voices sounded like Matt's. Though, clearly there were men other than Scottie and Reggie in there talking.

I entered the living room, "Ok now. Hey guys. I'm Johanna. You all looked so handsome today."

There was a chorus of hellos and thank yous.

After which I said, "now about the wedding..."

Scottie said, "Man, I'm not even gonna talk about that shit."

"Look you need to whisper," said Shante.

"Whisper? Why whisper?" I asked. Shante pointed at Reggie.

He went on to whisper, "because the honeymoon suite is right next door!"

I wish I could've seen the look on my own damn face. "Oh my god! Are they in there?"

Everybody replied at once, "YES!"

"Reggie," everyone looked at me. "I have to ask you something."

"Yes?" The heads turned to look at him.

"Did you ever find any chicken for the reception?" The laughter was uncontrollable. I don't think I ever got an actual response for that question either.

There was so much laughter and love in that room. Scottie and Shante. Reggie and Cheryl. Anthony and his cousin. Someone named Thomas. Matt came up, eventually. Then there was me. I knew that we were all sitting together talking but it wasn't until I saw my reflection in the window. I watched the smile form on my face. Yeah, I was ok or, at least, I was damn close to it.

I felt the need to wrap up the evening with a toast, "Although the day was long and arduous, we all made it through. It is important that we recognize the intention of love, the intention of Adam and Alicia. We must leave this moment knowing that they said, "I do," in their own way and in their own time. Believe it or not, we were extremely fortunate to bear witness to the occasion. So, to new love, to the bride and groom, to friendship and hope, to finding love in yourself, in your own way and in your own time. Cheers."

Joycelyn Wells

HELL TO PAY

The girls and I spent Sunday at the pool. It was slow moving and lazy due to most of the guests checking out. We had Javier to ourselves for the most part and Lucia continued to take care of us poolside. We made plans to get coins before morning. We needed to make our final wishes before we hit the road.

Everyone was gone, including Anthony. I was a bit saddened by that because we never actually had a conversation. I realized that in all the time I had been married, I never noticed a man noticing me. Is it that it hasn't happened before or was I just blind to it? Though a better question may be, why can I see it now?

My thoughts were lazy and free as I chilled by the pool. My girls were having a good time and that was alright with me.

When we arrived back to the penthouse Sunday evening, Matt was there watching TV. I tensed at the sight of him. I was over his nasty attitude and yucky tone. I convinced myself to just continue to do what I had been doing. Casually, he said, "Hey Babe. Y'all want to get some dinner?" There's no fucking way he was talking to me. I kept walking. "Jo, did you hear me?"

"No, I didn't. What did you say?"

"We haven't been out together since we arrived, y'all want to go get some dinner?"

What the fuck? I simply replied, "no, we had dinner already."

His tone was so kind and soothing. "Why didn't you tell me that you guys were going to get something to eat?"

"I didn't know that you wanted to know." I left the room.

"Ok, girls, it's bath time. We have an early day tomorrow and a long drive home." We followed our usual routine. After our baths, we read a few stories. I stayed up to pack most of our stuff then settled into bed with the girls. Matt was still sitting on the sofa when I closed the door.

It took me a few minutes to stop the racing thoughts. I didn't want him to be mad. What if he genuinely wanted to hang out with us? Then I asked myself, "Self? Do you want to hang out with him?" The answer was no. The more I thought about Matt the less I felt. His behavior over these last few months clearly shows that there's no place in his life for us anymore. *Was it ever? Am I trying to force a space for us?*

On another note, the weekend served me well. People saw me. I felt beautiful. I was referred to as beautiful. I have laughed and played and even been a tad bit spontaneous. With those realizations, I turned over and went to sleep.

There was no need to set an alarm or anything. We wouldn't sleep past 8am and check-out wasn't until noon. We would take our time and get on the road when we were ready. I believe Matt slept in the other room. I'm not sure but he was sulking and didn't say anything to any of us all morning. But his bags were by the door, he would be ready whenever we were. He's trying to show me that he's good Matt today.

His behavior is so predictable. It never fails, whenever he shows out, he spends the day pouting and playing the victim. If I don't respond to that then he'll want to start a fight. He'll do anything to get some attention from me. Then immediately after the fight, he wants to be my friend. What a vicious cycle. Though not today, I am not arguing at all. I will not be suckered into his manipulation. He would have to tough this out on his own.

At check out, I requested my van from valet. Javier was working, so we were able to say good-bye. He even had some coins ready for us. Which was perfect because I forgot to get some on yesterday, even though that was my on my list of things to do. While we waited, we went over to the fountain to make our farewell wishes.

This time my wish was more specific, not only did I want happiness, but I also wanted to be comfortable with being happy.

Matt's voice interrupted my thought, "the van is ready."

I kissed my coin and tossed it in the fountain. "Ok girls are y'all ready to hit the road."

"Yes, Mommy."

"Yes."

"Good, let's hit it."

We held hands as we exited the hotel. The valet attendant put our bags in and opened the sliding door for the girls. I walked around to the driver's side and put my purse in the seat then buckled Janise and her baby into the car seat. Matt was standing by the driver's door looking at my purse, like it was in his way.

I walked back to the driver's side. "Excuse me. I'm driving." Matt just stood there. I repeated myself. "I'm driving... home."

He was trying to find the right thing to say. Eventually, he asked, "why?" I knew it. Classic Matt.

Did his question deserve an answer? I obliged. "Because I don't want to ride in silence. I'd like to enjoy my girls and the music along the way. And, mainly because, I enjoy driving."

He walked around to the passenger side and got in.

"Jacquelyn, are you buckled?"

"Yes."

"Awesome. Theeennnn L E T S G O."

The girls were singing our chant as we drove out of the parking lot. Once we hit the highway, I turned on the radio. We sang and danced in our seats until it was time to stop for a bathroom break. Matt continued to sit there.

"Jo, we really need to talk."

"Do we Matt? About what? Hold that thought." He didn't have to hold it. He could fucking forget it! Who gives a damn what he did with it? "I want to go to the bathroom first?"

Back on the road, the music filled the van while the girls and I chatted about any and everything. I didn't address the 'we need to talk' until the girls fell asleep. I hated to argue or get flustered in front of them, so I waited.

"Ok, Matt, what do you want to talk about?"

"Anthony."

"What about him?"

He looked at me. "What was going on between you two?"

I laughed. "Matt, are you serious?"

"Yes."

Now, ain't this some bullshit? This motherfucker has shown absolutely no regard for anything or anybody but himself for months. Now, he wants to question me about something that's nothing.

"Oh, in that case, nothing."

"If it was nothing, why was he trying to introduce you to me?"

"The bigger question is why weren't you trying to introduce your wife to your" I used my fingers to do air quotes, "good friend"?

"Don't try to turn this around on me."

"Wow."

"I'm serious Jo. I think it's kinda funny that of all the women there he chose you to introduce to me.

"Well, he did say that I looked beautiful."

"Oh, so now you are just trying to make me mad."

"Mad? Why would you get mad? Hell, maybe I should be mad because the compliment didn't come from my husband."

"Do I have to say it for you to know it?"

"Whatever Matt, you don't have to say anything else to me ever."

"Bet you'll talk to that lame ass muthafucker if he wants to talk to you."

"Maybe..."

"Keep on Jo, let me find out something was going on and there's gonna be hell to pay."

"Who's going to pay it?"

"You."

"Let me get this straight, instead of asking your quote unquote good friend about whatever you think this is, you are going to try to bully your wife into admitting some shit that didn't happen? Why because your friendships are more valuable than your marriage? Matt, I'm not doing this with you." I turned the radio up.

He turned the radio down. "Doing what with me?"

"Arguing about whatever this is."

His voice softened. "I'm not trying to argue Jo. I'm just worried about us."

"As you should be." I turned the music up again.

We rode for another hour or so before he spoke again. This time he was big mad. He had sat in that seat and replayed my words over and over. He knew this was fucked up, but he would never admit it. All he had to do was say, "damn, Jo, I've been a whole ass lately. I'm sorry." But no, he reached over and grabbed my arm. I didn't pull away. I just glared at him and said, "kill yourself if you want but you will not take me and my girls with you. Now, release my arm."

"Jo, you think I'm fucking playing with you. I'm serious, there's going to be..."

He released my arm and glared at me.

"Yes, I know. Hell to pay! I feel like I'm already paying it."

"What do you mean by that?"

"Look how you are treating me; I'm your wife and you act like you don't even know me. You'd prefer to be up somebody else's ass rather than spend any amount of time with me."

"That's not true."

"Boy stop, I..." I caught myself, I refused to engage in this raggedy ass conversation. "No comment."

"No comment?"

"Nada. None. Zilch."

We were quiet for several miles. I spoke first. "Look Matt, I'm trying to find some happiness. You cannot ruin that for me. You've made your wants clear... loud and clear. So, I've gotta find something for me outside of us."

"What do you mean by that?"

"I'm no longer begging you to do... anything. I will respect your movements."

"Jo, that doesn't sound right."

"To whom?"

"Listen, if you...

I cut him off. "I know, I know, hell to pay, blah, blah, blah."

"See there you go with the jokes."

"Maybe, but now that I think about it, hell to pay doesn't sound so bad." I looked over at him and laughed, "I mean really, our whole relationship has suffered drastically due to you getting caught up in that damn wedding and the reception slash wake."

It took him a moment to process my words. Once he thought about it, I saw a smile creep upon his face then laughter. "Wow, Jo, you have to admit that shit was crazy, right?"

"As hell... whoever heard of *Death by A Wedding?*"

For the first time in years, we had a whole conversation, that had nothing to do with us, laughter and tears included. Now he thinks we are friends again. Maybe, though there is quite a difference. While, Matt is for Matt, please believe, Jo is definitely for Jo.

Joycelyn Wells

More from our great authors:

Bottom of the Map
Steven L. Brown

Arrow Spell: Collection of Poetry
David Ciceron

I Am The Child of a King &
The Daughter of a Queen
Sharon Guthrie Johnson

She's Unmoved
Tiffany Mitchell

The Evolution of Poetry
Krystal Orellano

Poetic Opulence
George Patterson

Loss of Innocence
Al B. Richards

Children's Collection

Luka Loves the Light
Fartema Fagin

Imagine A Place
Ashley Rogers

Made in the USA
Columbia, SC
24 August 2022